Choosing Joy

In His Choosing
Book 2

By

Ronna M. Bacon

Philippians 4:4 Be strong and of a good courage, fear not, nor be afraid of them: for the   Rejoice in the Lord always. Again I will say, rejoice!

Psalm 16:1 You will show me the path of life; In your presence is fullness of joy; At Your right hand are pleasures forevermore

NKJV

Table of Contents

Chapter 1

Twilight was dropping onto the downtown area of the city of Toronto, Ontario. It didn't darken the area much. There was just too much artificial light. The man leaning against a brick building was alert even though he seemed to be relaxed and not interested in any of the pedestrians scurrying by him, heading for both the subway and the nearby buses. His deep blue eyes searched the mass of people, looking for one particular female. He had memorized her looks. Told that she was in the area, he had headed that way earlier that day, desperate to find her. He felt the danger that she was in and knew that he could not live with himself if he could prevent any harm coming to her. His heart raised in prayer for a successful search. God was in control of the situation, not him. He needed to wait for God to show him the female.

Shifting on his sneaker-clad feet, Roane Monaghan was not even sure if the source had been correct in their words to him. He didn't want to walk away if there was a chance that she was there. He could feel the evil in the air around him and that frightened him to some extent. He was not one who frightened easily, given his work as a private investigator, but there were times when that did happen. This early evening dusk was one of those times.

Roane tugged his ball cap further down over his face, covering his dark brown hair. He didn't want to be recognized, not that there was likely much chance of that. This was just how he was. He went in and out on investigations, keeping as low a profile as he could. This time? There was more at stake than just him.

On the move, Roane had spotted his quarry. He shifted through the crowds of hurrying humanity, reaching the female, no lady, he decided. His hand reached for her wrist, drawing her with him. He could feel the resistance that she was putting up and he couldn't say that he blamed her, a stranger grabbing hold of her and tugging her away from where she had been walking.

The lady dug in her heels, not wanting to go with a man whom she didn't know. This sudden grasp on her wrist had frightened her. She had felt watched for too many days and weeks but couldn't find the person who was responsible. Ragen Osborne had been on the run for days now, leaving everything she had behind except for what she could pack into the black backpack she wore. Not that there had been much. She had been on the streets since her teens, trying had to work her way up in her chosen field of laboratory medicine. That hadn't been working out so well lately. She had taken a leave from her employer, not sure that she would ever return to that lab.

"Let me go!" Her voice hissed at the man who kept a tight hold on her despite how much she twisted at her wrist. "Let me go!"

Roane nodded to himself. She was reacting just as she should, having a stranger grab at her. She just kept moving with him as he tugged her harder towards the entrance to the subway. Paying their fares, Roane didn't head for the train. Instead, he kept them moving through the throngs of people, his eyes on an exit down the platform from them. He simply tightened his hold on the lady and kept her moving with him despite her pleas to release her.

"I need to get you out of here. Someone was following you and meant you harm." Roane's deep voice was kept low, just loud enough for Ragen to hear him. He shot her a quick look, seeing the shock and then acceptance on her face. "I promise. We'll talk. For now, we're heading for that exit." His finger jabbed at that direction. "Then, we're catching a bus. I was hired to find you. Only, I don't know if that person meant to save you or harm you. And I have been caught in the middle."

Ragen was shocked at his words. There was no one who would do that. All of her family was gone, at least those that she knew. There may be other relatives but she had chosen to walk away from her hometown up in the northern part of the province of Ontario and settle in the southern portion. Only that didn't seem to be that great of a choice at the moment.

Their steps now matching in time, Roane hustled Ragen from the subway and towards where a bus was waiting. He had already purchased tickets on it, heading for a town near his own home town. He had left his car in the safety of a friend's driveway, hoping and praying that God would lead him quickly to his quarry. And He had. It was up to Roane now to determine just what was going on and to bring Ragen to safety.

His steps slowed as he approached the bus depot. It too was busy with passengers and pedestrians.

—

Roane could still feel the danger that had lingered all day, dogging his path as he searched for Ragen. He paused for a moment, Ragen trying hard to catch her breath before he was tugging her forward once more and then shoving her up the steps into the bus. Their tickets were handed over before he was shoving her down the bus aisle to a seat at the very back.

Ragen slumped onto the seat for a moment, her wrist free from Roane's grip but she still felt as if she was a prisoner. The tall handsome man who had dragged her away from the subway entrance had slid in beside her, blocking her from leaving. Her deep brown eyes studied him as she tugged at her blond hair caught back in a braid. This was not what she had expected to happen. She had planned on finding a bed in the local shelter and then leaving Toronto for another town. She just didn't know which one.

"Can you explain?" Ragen kept her voice low, not wanting any other passenger to step in.

"I can. For now, my name is Roane Monaghan. I'm a private investigator who was hired to find you." Roane's identification was out and handed over to her.

Ragen stared at him in shock. This was not what she had expected to her. She had feared the worst.

"A private investigator? But why? And who?" Ragen wanted, no demanded, an answer right then and there.

"We'll talk. I promise you that. But first, we need to get out of Toronto and to where I have my car. I don't mean you any harm." Roane's eyes were searching outside of the bus windows, not seeing

—

anyone who stood out but then again the area was packed with people on their way to wherever it was they were headed. And all of them were strangers to him. He tucked his wallet back into his pocket, sensing that Ragen would question him and question him thoroughly. It was what Roane would have done.

"Oh, we'll talk all right." Ragen's body slumped with sudden fatigue. She had not been sleeping well, if at all, and this adrenaline rush had sapped what little strength she had left. As the bus moved through the traffic in the city towards the major highways, Ragen's head slid sideways to be cushioned against Roane's shoulder as she slept.

Roane stared down at her, shocked in some ways that she was asleep, but grateful that their conversation would now take place in private. God was here, he knew, and in control, guiding Roane as he had moved through the past few days with planning his steps and then bringing Ragen to his attention.

His eyes in constant movement, Roane kept watch over the lady beside him, knowing that someone on the bus meant them harm. He could feel the evil near him. That sort of feeling had saved him many times in the past when he was out for work. Roane didn't like that sense of evil but he was too much of a realist not to know that God was there and that He had angels around them right now to protect them.

Glancing at his watch, Roane sighed. He needed to wake the lady but he wasn't sure how she would react. That was the unknown right now. If she screamed and fought him, then he would end up under arrest and that was definitely not in his plans for the evening. In fact, Roane had no idea what his plans were for the evening. He had thoughts about what to do. Only, circumstances could and would likely change that.

His head had tilted a number of times over the course of the hours that they had been on the bus, studying the lady beside him. She had not roused, despite the bumps and swaying of the bus. He sighed to himself once more. He needed to wake her but was unsure just how to do that. Roane finally reached for Ragen's hand and squeezed it gently.

"Miss Osborne? I need you to wake up. We're almost at our destination." Roane waited for a moment before his mouth opened to repeat his words. That wasn't necessary.

—

Ragen stirred, sensing that she was somewhat safe. She just didn't know where she was. She felt the movement of the bus and frowned before her eyes opened to the barest of slits and she gazed around. It was true, she decided. Ragen was on a bus, with a stranger, heading for who knew where and just what she would find there, that was the unknown.

"I'm awake." Her voice was grumpy, causing Roane to bite back a grin. "Just where are we?"

"Miles from Toronto and almost to my town. I parked my car in the town we're entering now early this morning. I hope to find it and get you to further safety." Roane watched the passengers carefully, knowing that once the bus stopped and they were disembarking, that became a dangerous point for Ragen.

"Your town? Who said I was going there?" Ragen was becoming combative. The danger and the uncertainty of what she was facing caused that. She felt safe and protected with Roane. Ragen just didn't understand that. She had not felt that way for years.

"I do. I need to keep you safe. I have a detective friend who will investigate what has been going on and before you say anything, I know that something has. Tell me I'm wrong." Roane waited patiently even as he felt the bus slow and then stop.

Ragen shrugged, her eyes searching the passengers. He was here, wasn't he, the one who had been chasing her? Or else he had hired someone to be here. But how did he know where she was and that

—

12

Roane would pull her onto a bus to leave Toronto. Those had not been her plans, she decided.

"No, you're not wrong. I just don't know who or why. I have sensed someone around me for the past few years. It's scares me, Mr. Monaghan, and that is not something that I like to feel." She sniffed, unable to control the tears that flooded her eyes. There was a sense of relief that she had someone to whom she could at last speak with.

Roane's eyes slid shut for a moment before he was on his feet, her backpack over his shoulder, and his hand reaching to draw her to her feet. Ragen protested slightly at that before she shrugged. She would grant him that bit of protection for now. It wouldn't last. Ragen knew that she would soon be on her own and on her way to somewhere else. She just didn't understand the character of the man who walked them from the bus and then around to the back of it, to disappear into the darkness.

Roane was distressed and saddened at her words. He had grown up in a noisy but loving family and had friends who stood shoulder to shoulder to him when they needed to, just as he did with them. He suddenly wanted his friends to be there for Ragen and he knew that they would be. They had been there for Slavin and Shaye when they went through their adventure not that long ago.

"No, that is something that no one should feel, particularly a beautiful lady such as yourself. I would like to help you, if I may." Roane didn't stop moving, tugging Ragen with him as he did so, finding a small diner that he entered before he shoved her onto a bench

---

seat and then slid onto it beside her. Danger was near them, he could feel it.

Ragen stared at him in disbelief for a moment before she shrugged. She would grant him this evening. She would be moving on either that night or the next morning. Ragen just didn't understand that Roane would never let her do that. He had become invested in protecting her and would put his life on the line to do so. He felt God's hand on them as he made that commitment, first to God, secondly albeit unspoken to Ragen, and then to himself.

Their meal in front of them, Roane stared down at his. He was not really that hungry but knew that he had to eat just to ensure that Ragen did. He felt sure that she was not eating regularly but she would never admit to that. Not yet, any way. And he had no intention of letting her walk away from him.

"May I call you Ragen?" Roane kept his voice low. He didn't want anyone in the diner to suspect that they were not friends. And if that happened, he could be in a lot of trouble with the authorities.

Ragen stared at him and then nodded, simply asking if she could call him Roane. She gave a small smile at his nod, not sure where they were heading but knowing somehow that Roane would do his best to protect her.

"Where are we heading, Roane? You just said a friend's place. I need to know where that is and if I'm safe." Ragen would not back away from him.

"We will head there after we eat." Roane hesitated for a moment. "If I can retrieve my car, we'll

———

head for my town. I have an apartment in my basement that you are welcome to use at no cost." He grinned for a moment once more as she stared at him. "I don't charge people to use it. It's kept for people in need or those needed short-term housing."

"Where have you been all of my life, Roane? Do you know what this means?" Ragen blinked, not wanting to let the tears flow. She knew that if she did, they would never stop. And that she didn't want, not out here in public.

Chapter 3

Roane hesitated as he approached his friend's home, Ragen's hand still tight in his. He had not let go of it despite her protests that he do so. Her backpack was once more over his shoulder. Roane frowned at his car before he quickly headed that way, unlocking it and shoving Ragen inside. He was on his knees, inspecting it and fully expecting to find trackers or worse a bomb. He found nothing.

Behind the wheel, Roane started his car and then hesitated. He needed to drive home but something was keeping him from doing that. He sighed. God was preventing him from driving off. Roane had had that in the past and had learned early to follow those nudges.

"Ragen? I need to drive off but God is stopping me from heading for home. Where do we go?" Roane was troubled, to say the least. It wasn't right that he was still out here with Ragen and faced the possibility that this would take all night. That would not help her reputation. Roane wanted to preserve that at all costs.

Ragen shrugged. She had no idea what to say or where to tell him to go. This was not an area that she knew.

"You need to go home, Roane. Just drive off." She stared out of the window, not seeing the shocked look that he sent her.

Roane backed out of the driveway, knowing that she was correct. He chose to drive through random

—

streets in that town before he headed for a back route that he was familiar with. Roane suspected that he was being watched and prayed that he had lost whoever it was and that whoever it was would take the highway. The route that he had chosen would take a bit longer but he didn't sense that God was stopping him from going that way.

Ragen studied the man driving the vehicle. She was not afraid of him, not like she had been afraid of any other man who might have stepped in to help her. She had been afraid of what they would ask in return. Roane was different. He didn't seem to want anything other than to keep her safe and find out what had happened to cause him to search her out.

"Roane? Are we safe?" Ragen's voice was quiet and hesitant. She felt God in the car with them but she was too much of a realist not to know that He could and would allow events to happen, even if it was their death.

"As safe as we can be for now." Roane's foot was steady on the accelerator pedal. His eyes were in constant motion, searching for someone who meant them harm. "I'm heading for my house, Ragen. If you would consider staying in the apartment at least for tonight, I would be grateful. Then we can reconsider what you do after that. I don't want to see you hurt and that is exactly what I fear will happen if you disappear."

"Thank you, Roane. No one has ever done this for me. My father? I have no idea where he is. I have never seen him. He left my mother when I was just a few months old and she never said why. My mother?

———

I had to leave when I was sixteen. I couldn't handle the lifestyle that she began to live - the drugs, the alcohol, and everything that came with it. I hit the streets but still managed to graduate from high school and then college." Ragen was sober as she spoke, knowing that Roane would poke until he had all the details that she was willing to share.

"I'm sorry, Ragen. I am so sorry that your life was like that. God blessed me with a caring and loving family. They'll take you in." Roane didn't doubt for one moment that they would refuse to do help her. It was not who they were.

"They would do that? How many are in your family any way?" Ragen didn't really want to know. She just couldn't handle the silence if they didn't talk.

"In my family? I have two brothers and two sisters as well as my parents. My grandparents on both sides are still with us. I also have aunts and uncles and many cousins. I am sure that they will all want to meet you." Roane didn't continue. He couldn't put into words that he hoped and prayed that Ragen stayed in his life forever. She was working her way into his heart even on such short notice.

"That's a lot of people. I have no idea if I have any family other than my parents. My mother never talked about them, and my father just wasn't there." Ragen stared out at the darkness, lit only by the lights from the occasional vehicle that passed them or from random houses that had lights on outside or shining through their windows.

—

Roane shot her a quick glance, watching her face in the dim light coming from the dashboard. He sighed. This was not how this was to go down. Roane was to find the lady and then get her to safety. His feelings were not to become involved and they had. He couldn't walk away from her, not at all. God was leading in this. Roane just wasn't sure where it was heading or just how dangerous it would become.

Pulling to a stop down the street from his house, Roane hesitated to drive up to it. He wasn't sure why but God was stopping him. He glanced at Ragen who was staring at him and then out of the windshield.

"Roane? Aren't you going to your home? It is on this street, isn't it?" Ragen was suddenly afraid that the man who was beside her could not be trusted.

"I am. There is something off there." Roane reached for his phone. "John? Are you on duty?"

"I am. You're calling me, Roane. What's happening?" John headed for his patrol vehicle, knowing full well that Roane was not calling him just because. Not at that time of night.

"I was away all day and am now parked down the street from my home. I can't go towards it. I have a friend with me that I am trying to protect." Roane didn't have to say anything more. He knew John would understand. This was not the first time that the two friends had worked together to protect someone.

"I see. Stay put. I have a key to your home. I'll walk around it and then through it. I'll find you. I would suggest that you drive off and find a diner somewhere." John paused, not sure what was happening with Roane. He was afraid that whatever it was that one of their other friends, Slavin, had gone through with his now wife, Shaye, had now turned its attention to Roane.

Roane pocketed his phone, his hand reaching for Ragen's as he prayed for them. Ragen was not sure what was happening other than that she was exhausted, hungry, and just wanted to go home. And she no longer had that home to go to.

Chapter 4

Parking at a nearby coffee shop, Roane reached for Ragen's hand, bending his head to pray for her and the situation that she now found herself in. He had no idea where it was heading, other than he didn't and wouldn't walk away from the beautiful lady seated in his car. He looked up at last, to find Ragen studying him.

"Why are you doing this, Roane? You don't know me. I could be a criminal pretending to be in trouble." Ragen bit at her lip, not sure what she really wanted to ask. All she could do was pray that God heard her and answered her unspoken prayer for someone to step in and protect her.

"Why am I doing this? First, because you need someone in your corner to protect you. Secondly, you are a sister in Christ. I cannot and will not walk away from you. It's not how we as Christians are to act or show our commitment to one another in God." Roane paused, not sure how to continue.

"In other words, you're being the hands and feet for God on earth." Ragen sighed. "And you just won't leave, will you, no matter how dangerous it gets."

"No, I won't, Ragen. That is a promise that I am making to you. As long as I have breath, I will be there for you." Roane kept his eyes on her, seeing as she finally nodded. "God is here, Ragen, even though it seems as if He is not. He is protecting us. We may not like what we have to go through but He does not allow

---

anything to happen to us that is not in His will for us. I have a friend who just went through danger with his now wife. We'll track them down tomorrow and you can talk with both Slavin and Shaye." Roane's eyes went to the window as he heard a vehicle and nodded at John before John slipped into the back seat, startling Ragen who stared at him with huge, fear-filled eyes.

"Who are you?" Ragen's voice shook with her fear, higher pitched that it normally was. She felt threatened, not necessarily by the man in the back seat but someone was out there and who meant her harm.

"I'm John, a police detective. And also a friend. If you're a friend of Roane's, then you're a friend of mine." He continued to grin even as he held up his identification. "I understand that you're the one that Roane called me about."

"I guess that I am. I don't know who is after me. That scares me, do you know that?" Ragen was becoming combative. She was exhausted, terrified, and found herself in a town that she didn't know. She had no idea where she could go to hide, even if she was able to get away from Roane.

"We'll work on that for you, Ragen, if I may call you that." John waited patiently for her to think through his words and then nod. He studied her closely, seeing the fear that she was trying hard to hide, the dark shadows under her eyes that meant a lack of sleep, and the tension that oozed from her. His eyes then studied his friends, seeing the caring and concern that he was feeling for the lady in his car. John frowned for a moment. Roane's attitude was different this time. John sighed to himself. Another friend off on another adventure that would drag in all his friends. And because Roane had contacted him, John would likely be the investigating detective.

The sudden glare of multiple lights through the windows of Roane's car startled the three. John reached for his weapon, ready to defend them when the doors were violently wrenched open. The three occupants were hurriedly pulled from the vehicle, hands on Roane and Ragen holding them in place. John's hands were in the air as he was forced to stand behind his vehicle, his eyes trying their best to study their assailants and remember what he could. He didn't see the upraised weapon held by the man behind him and had no chance to avoid the heavy hammering of it down onto his head. John collapsed without a word, a scream from Ragen the only sound in the night air.

The men shot quick looks around the area before Roane was shoved into a truck and Ragen into another. The men drove off, not quickly so as not to arouse any suspicion. Roane twisted on his seat, trying to see behind him but unable to in the darkness of the night despite the lights in the parking lot. He feared for his friend and prayed that John was still alive. There were no guarantees that he was and that worried Roane to a great extent.

Ragen bit down hard on her lip, drawing blood from it. She was sandwiched between two men, strangers to her that meant harm to her and also Roane. Ragen worried about John as well, not seeing him shoved towards a vehicle after he had been shoved behind his own. Was he even still alive? And just

———

where was God in all this? Wasn't He supposed to protect them and prevent this? Her thoughts tumbled over one another and she was unable to pray at this point, her fear just too great.

Consternation swirled through the police department as Jerome, another detective, searched the building for John. He had been scheduled to return to go over cases with Jerome and hadn't appeared. A search began for him, ending at the parking lot where his car still sat. Roane's car had disappeared, leaving no trace of why John would have been there. This had been well planned, that much was obvious to those who had orchestrated it.

Jerome's hand reached to rest on John's back, grateful for the rise and fall of it as John breathed. His head tilted as he studied the bloody lump on the back of John's head. He had been ambushed, Jerome decided, but why was he here? Had he been meeting with someone?

A patrol officer ran towards Jerome, bringing him to his feet and moving that way.

"What do you have, Jack?" Jerome's hand stopped the officer.

"John was meeting with someone. I can't tell who. And the plate isn't clear. We can see trucks moving in and a man and woman were shoved into them. John had already gone down at that point." Jack was worried. A fellow officer was down, a couple were missing, and they had no idea who or why yet.

"A couple?" Jerome spun to stare back to where the paramedics were working on a still unconscious

---

John. "I wonder. Jack? Head towards Roane's home and see if his car is there. If it is, talk to him. I heard from him earlier today that he had headed out of town to find someone. And if that someone was with him and they've disappeared, we're now on a time crunch to find them." He walked back towards John's car, a word to a fellow officer to retrieve a copy of the video feed. It was now evidence in a kidnapping and an assault on a fellow officer.

Chapter 5

John roused slowly hours later, disoriented as to where he was and why. A hand felt at the back of his head as he sat up slowly on the hospital stretcher. His eyes were narrowed as he glanced around, the lights almost too bright for him. His head pounded as he lifted it, staring at Jerome as that man spoke with him.

"What was that, Jerome?" John slid slowly from the stretcher, a hand resting on it until he regained the smallest sense of balance.

"You were found behind your car in a diner parking lot. Who were you meeting?" Jerome's hand went out to John's arm to help him balance as John shuffled slowly towards the exit.

"I was? I think it was Roane and the lady that he found. A Ragen Osborne. From what little he had time to tell me, he had been asked to find her. When he did, he felt compelled to bring her here, to protect her. Roane didn't have a good feeling about who had asked him to find her." John's steps stopped as his eyes closed. The headache was growing worse.

"He was? That makes sense. But his car wasn't there. And it's not at his home. We've already checked that out." Jerome was puzzled as well as worried about the other man. "What did he tell you about this lady?"

"We didn't have a lot of time to talk. I had just met them when we were pulled from his car. I was taken down right away. I have no idea where he is."

John stared at the young man standing in front of him. "Rowan? You're here?"

"I am, John. Roane said that he had reached out to you." Rowan frowned at John. He was Roane's oldest brother, the eldest of the five children in the family. "You don't look so good."

"He's not. He was hit over the head when Roane and the lady with him disappeared." Jerome continued to urge John forward.

"A lady? Is that what he was up to today? He didn't say. Not that he will when he's involved in an investigation. But that doesn't explain where he is. I can't find him anywhere." Rowan paced with the two detectives, not willing to leave John without finding out all that he could. He was the eldest brother in Roane's family with their sister, Artis, next, then Roane, then their youngest brother, Ryley, and their youngest sister, Arin. They were a close-knit family, walking in and out of one another lives as they could but always surrounding each other in prayer.

"We can't either. John was assaulted he says as he met with Roane and a lady named Ragen. They've disappeared. We can't tell you what we have in evidence." Jerome studied Rowan before he was studying John. John was wavering on his feet. "John, you're with me tonight. No arguments."

John stared back at Jerome with one eye that was barely open, the other one closed. He was almost out on his feet and didn't know if he would make it to Jerome's without passing out again.

—

27

"I gathered that. Let me rest for a bit and we'll talk."

John walked unsteadily into Jerome's house, Rowan tailing the two detectives. He wasn't going anywhere until he had some answers and those answers were likely not to come any time soon if what Jerome had stated was true. All Rowan could do was to pray for his brother and whatever it was he had become mixed up in. He was well aware at times that Roane's work could be dangerous. The family had tried their best to talk him out of his chosen occupation. Roane had smiled, hugged each one, and then walked away, leaving them staring at him as he did so, silence left behind him.

Jerome watched Rowan as he worked around in his kitchen, a prayer raising for his friend and his friend's brother. The men were a close friend group, just expanding as the men had married. The wives had become friends as well with Rowan's female relatives.

"What can you tell me, Jerome? Is Roane okay?" Rowan leaned against the kitchen counter, not seeing the light marbling of the countertop. His arms folded across his chest as his head dropped for a moment.

"Not a lot. I'm sorry, Rowan. I wish that I could tell you more but it's just not possible. We can't tell from the video feed what happened. If Roane's car was there and we have no doubt that it was, it was blocked from view. We can see two trucks and a car drive away. We just don't know about who was in them." Jerome slid a cup of coffee towards Rowan, his head turning for a moment to listen for John. His head

---

shook against the thoughts that he had. Jerome could only thank their Heavenly Father that John was still alive, even though hurt.

"That's about what I thought you would say." Rowan stared down at the cup he held. "I don't know what to tell the family. Mom had called, just asking if I had heard from Roane. She had this premonition that something has happened to him. And those feelings of hers are usually correct."

"I know that they are. We've discussed that, your mother and I." Jerome slumped back against the white fridge for a moment, exhausted. There were just too many cases for them to investigate and that bothered him.

"I'm off then, Jerome." Rowan rinsed out his cup and set it to one side. "Call me if you find out anything. I'll take the calls for the family." He walked away, the white steel front door with the large decorative window closing behind him. Rowan stood beside his car, his eyes on his keys before he was in it and driving towards Roane's. He was out of the car and walking around the house before he entered it and searched, not finding his brother anywhere there. Rowan stood for a moment, tears briefly clouding his eyes as he worried about his brother before he began to pray for Roane. He had no idea what Roane was facing but he was afraid that Roane was going through what Slavin and Shaye had done. That scared him.

The men watching the house shared a glance. This was not Roane who had appeared. They were under orders to find him and bring them to their boss.

That obviously was not happening that night. Who knew when it might happen.

Chapter 6

Groaning as he rolled to his side from his stomach, Roane's hand found his ribs. He was extremely sore there, he knew, from the assault that he had undergone. He had no idea who had kidnapped him and Ragen and that he wanted to know. He groaned again as he managed to sit up, an arm wrapped around his chest. His eyes searched the room or what he could see of it in the dim light. Struggling to his feet and biting at his lip to keep the groans inside him, Roane stood for a moment before he began a systematic search of the room, not finding anything that explained where he was or why. He also found nothing that he could use as a weapon.

His eyes on the door, Roane hesitated to walk that way, fully expecting to find the door locked. His surprise when the knob turned and the door opened coloured his face. He stopped for a moment, his face raising to the ceiling as he prayed, asking permission to leave the room. Not finding that God was stopping him, Roane stepped through, surprise on his face once more as he entered a large living area. He frowned, turning slowly in a circle. This was not what he had expected, not at all. A sound to his right had him stopping in his turn before he looked that way.

Ragen stood there, fear on her face as she watched Roane. She had been threatened with her own assault if she tried anything. Fear had kept her from responding, worry about Roane uppermost in her mind. He had struggled to get to her and had been beaten to some extent before his body was dragged from the room and just dumped in the bedroom. Ragen almost ran towards Roane to be swept into a hug, one that she returned, not feeling the way that Roane was holding himself so that he didn't respond in pain to her tight hug.

"Ragen? You're okay?" Roane kept his voice low, not knowing if they were alone or not.

"I am. You're not." Ragen looked up at the tall handsome man holding her. "We need to get out of here. Do you know where we are?"

"I do and yes, we do. Are there any of the men around?" Roane nudged her towards the door.

"No, they left after threatening us. Can we get away?" Ragen reached to unlock the door, praying as she did that there were no dogs out there or someone still around who would stop them.

"I pray that we can. I know where we are. We're not really that far from my home." Roane's hand reached for Ragen's, finding that she was reaching for his. "This way." Roane walked as quickly as he could away from the house and towards the sidewalk, carefully watching for anyone who would prevent them from walking away.

"We're that close to your home? I thought that we were miles away from it." Ragen's voice was barely a whisper.

"No, they drove us around town, I think to try and confuse us. I know this town too well." Roane hesitated as he saw lights on in his house and then recognized the car in the driveway. "Rowan's here. He's been looking for us." He led Ragen quickly to the back door and inside the house, startling Rowan as he did so. "Rowan?"

"Roane? You're okay?" Rowan reached to hug his brother and then surprised Ragen by hugging here. "What happened?"

"I need to talk with John." Roane paced the kitchen, not seeing the look that Ragen was sending his way.

"You can't. He was knocked down and out. He's with Jerome. Let me reach out to Jerome." Rowan walked away to a spot where he could stand and watch his brother.

Roane nodded even as he worked to make the tea that he had learned Ragen liked before he reached for the coffee carafe.

"Jerome? Can you leave John for a bit?" Rowan kept his voice low.

"I can. Why?" Jerome simply locked his front door and headed for his car. "Roane?"

"He's home and is with a lady. He hasn't said anything as yet. He wanted to talk with John." Rowan finally pocketed his phone after sending a message to their mother. He stated in simple terms that Roane was home but seemed to be off on an adventure of some kind. Would his mother pass on the need to pray for their brother?

Jerome hesitated in the entryway to the house, not sure that he should be there but he needed to be.

—

33

His searching gaze found Roane and Raven as they huddled on the couch, not touching but close to one another. He sighed. This was not going to be easy, he knew, and he also knew that Roane would be hurting because John had been hurt while watching out for him. And that was exactly what John had been doing.

"Roane?" Jerome's quiet voice had Roane jumping in fear for a moment as he looked up to stare at the office.

"Jerome? You're here? Of course, you are. Rowan called you." Roane sat back, his hand finding his bruised ribs. "You want our statements."

"I need to get them, Roane. You know that." Jerome watched as Ragen rose and walked away, leaving Roane looking bewildered and lost for a moment. "Tell me what happened."

"What happened? We were pulled from my car and taken to this address." Roane almost threw the pice of paper towards Jerome that held the address. "I know who owns that house. I didn't think that he would be involved in anything like this but it appears that he may be. I was assaulted when I refused to let them separate Ragen from me. Ragen found me early this morning. We just walked out of the house. There didn't seem to be anyone around." Roane was puzzled by that fact. "And there should have been. So what really was going on?"

Jerome shrugged. He needed to speak with Ragen and that would be difficult, given how Roane was reacting towards her. There was something more going on between the couple, more than just an

---

investigation. His friend was now off on one of those adventures, Jerome decided, and had drawn in more than just his family. He was drawing in his friends. Slavin would want to be involved as would their friend, Nickol. And that meant the danger would just keep growing.

Ragen simply shook her head when she was asked if she knew the house.

"I'm not from here. Roane mentioned the name but it means nothing to me. I still don't understand why he was asked to find me. It's not making sense. I was on the run and I can't explain why. Roane found me in downtown Toronto and brought me here. Can you explain what's happening?" Ragen waited for Jerome to respond. When he didn't, she was on her feet and heading for the door that lead to the suite in the basement. For now, she would stay there. She acknowledged that God was in control and only wanted the best for her. At the moment, Ragen was having trouble finding joy in anything and that she needed to find. It was elusive, this joy, but she knew that God was in control and was protecting her. It was just that His protection might not be what she expected to have.

Chapter 7

Later that morning, Rowan turned to face his brother. He had not walked away, choosing instead to remain at Roane's. He could hear his parents' voices speaking with Ragen in the kitchen. She was not responding very much but that was understandable, Rowan decided.

"Roane? What are your plans?" Rowan waited patiently for Roane to respond. It was how it was with the brothers. They asked their questions and then just waited for an answer, no matter how long it would take.

Roane ran his hands through his hair, not sure how to respond.

"I don't know, Rowan, to tell you the truth. I felt God's nudge to get her out of Toronto yesterday. I know that someone was on the bus with us that meant her harm. We were heading here to see if she wanted to live in the suite for a while until I could dig into this more. And then last night happened. John called. He's hurting and off work for now. That's frustrating for everyone of us. I just don't know why they did what they did." Roane paced his living room, not taking in the comfortable furnishing, the wall art in the form of photos, or the soft colours that he had chosen to paint the walls or chosen for the drapes.

Ragen hesitated in the doorway, not sure if she should enter or not. Rowan nodded towards her, causing Roane to turn before he was in front of her, reaching for her hands, his grasp warm and just tight enough to make Ragen feel safe.

"Ragen? What's wrong?" Roane ducked his head to study the lady standing in front of him. That she was worried and scared was obvious. "What can I or my family do for you?"

"You've done plenty. I can't stay here, Roane. They know that you are here. I can't have you hurt again because of me." Ragen tugged at her hands, trying to release them from Roane's grasp. That man just didn't let go of them.

"You can stay here. Or you can stay with either one of my sisters or even my parents. We have really good security systems." Roane bit at his lip, his father watching his son closely, seeing how distraught Roane was and knowing that he was doing his best to hide that fact.

"I can't do that. I need to leave." Ragen again tugged at her hands, not finding Roane letting go of her.

"You can't. You're a material witness to an assault on a police officer." Roane shook his head at her, his eyes briefly filled with the pain of knowing that John had been assaulted because of them. "Jerome wants you to stay where he can find you. For now, that's here unless you choose to move in with my family. I don't think that you want to do just that."

"No, I'm too dangerous to do that." Ragen's full attention was on the man in front of her who seemed so determined to protect her. She couldn't remember having that at all. She also didn't hear the door open and other people walk in and then stand nearby, listening to the conversation going on around them.

Roane's siblings stared at him, catching his eye for a moment before his gaze went back to Ragen. He knew that he had their support. That went without saying. It was how his family was. Granted, none of them had ever been in the position that Roane now found himself, but it made no difference. He was well aware that they would want to be on the search. Given their different personalities and occupations, they would all see it from a different perspective and that was what was needed. Roane also had no doubt that his friends would become involved, including Peter who had a security team. Peter would just move his team in on the couple if he felt it was warranted and necessary.

"Ragen? All we want to do is to protect you and then find out why this has happened. You stated that you have felt followed for months?" Jerome had not yet left but needed to soon. "Talk to me."

"I can't. I don't know who or why. If I had, I would have confronted them." Ragen walked away, heading for the back deck where she found the solitude that she was searching for. She didn't realize that Roane's sisters had followed her and found seats nearby, their gaze on her but their hearts raising in prayer for this lady now in their brother's life. Roane had never acted this way with anyone else that they were aware of. This made Ragen special to them and they would do what they could to solve whatever this mystery was that they were now all involved in.

Ragen raised her head at last, not surprised to find herself with company. Her mouth opened and then snapped closed. She had no idea who these ladies were but they must be related to Roane.

"Hi. I'm Roane's older sister, Artis, and this is our younger sister, Arin. We want to help you, Ragen, if I may call you that." Artis waited patiently for Ragen to think through her words before that lady nodded. "We don't know you but I think that we will become friends. Roane is not walking away from you, not ever, we can tell. You have become a part of our family, whether you wished to or not." She stopped speaking, seeing the longing on Ragen's face. "Ragen?"

"Do you know how long I have waited to have someone say that to me? I didn't have that with my own family. They just didn't seem to want or need me. I left as soon as I could." Ragen swiped at the tears on her face, finding Arin moving in to hug her. "I'm sorry."

"Don't be sorry. Tears are healing. In fact, we are told that God bottles our tears. They are that important to Him, just as you are." Arin shared a look with her sister, knowing that their brothers had stopped just outside of the back door, watching out for the three ladies, Roane standing just in front of his two brothers. "You're exhausted, terrified, and have been through an ordeal that no one should go through. You need to sleep and then take some time to refresh not just your body but your spirit and soul as well. God sometimes calls us aside by whatever He has allowed in order for us to do just that."

Roane moved to sit on the table in the front of Ragen, his hands held out for her to take. She studied him before she reached for him, finding his head bowing as he prayed for just her. She was not used to that, Ragen decided, but it helped a lot to know someone was praying for her.

"Thank you, Roane. I'm sorry to be so much trouble." Ragen's face and voice was sober as she spoke.

"It's no trouble, Ragen. It would have been had you disappeared and not been found. That we want to prevent. For today? Just take the time you need to rest. The suite is ready for you or you could go with the girls. It's your choice. We won't make that for you. Not unless it is needed because you are in danger." Roane made that promise to Ragen as well as himself. He knew himself well enough to know that he wanted to just step in and protect her as he did his sisters. He couldn't do that. Ragen needed her freedom and solitude to recover.

Chapter 8

Ragen moved through the suite the next morning, reaching to open the fridge, staring at the selection of food that was in it. She hadn't known that someone had gone shopping for her, but they had. She would need to find that person, thank them, and then repay them. Somehow, Ragen doubted that she would be able to.

Knowing that Roane wasn't home was not a comfort to her. She needed to talk with him, to decide what she was to do, but that would have to wait. Her phone chiming startled her as she spun to stare at her phone that lay on the kitchen table. Ragen crept close to the table, a finger out to swipe across the phone face. She drew in a deep breath. It was Arin, just asking if she wanted some company. She was parked in Roane's driveway, if she did. If not, then it was okay.

Ragen almost ran to the driveway, desperate to find someone to talk to. Arin simply wrapped Ragen into a hug and then tucked her into her car.

"You need some stuff, don't you?" Arin grinned as Ragen gaped at her before that lady nodded.

"I do. I can't get a lot. I'm not working right now." Ragen was saddened by that, knowing that at the present time, she just couldn't work and bring danger to anyone else.

"That's okay. I have some money that was given to me just for you." Arin waited patiently for Ragen to reach for the money. "We have friends who have a

———

charity that reaches out to those in need. They do this to be encouragers. I was contacted last night by one of them. They always know when someone has a need. God leads them in this."

Ragen stuttered out a response, not quite sure what she had said, and tucked the money into her purse. She stared at the house, knowing that she felt at home there but that would not last. She didn't have a home anywhere, not any more.

"I don't have a home, Arin. How do I live? I need to work but how do I do that?" Ragen was just speaking her mind, lost in thought as she was. She was not surprised when Arin simply prayed for her

"Roane needs help in his office. His paperwork is always behind. He'll employ you. If he doesn't, I know that Dad can use some help in his office. He runs a business that helps those in need. He's so busy now that he's working long hours to cope, despite Mom working there and the rest of us pitching in as we can. Do you want to head there? And before you ask, the office door is locked at all times except when someone in need comes in. And that is only to the front of the building. He is very careful that way." Arin once more waited for Ragen to respond.

"He would do that? I don't understand." Ragen studied the younger woman, not sure how to respond.

"He would. He calls it being the hands and feet for God on earth. And he has helped many people over the years. It's how we were raised. Our friends don't understand it but it is our family." Arin drove away, waving at Roane as she did so.

Roane stared after his sister's car before he spun his steering wheel and followed her. He frowned for a moment that Ragen was with her before he shrugged. He would find out what was up when he caught up to them. A motion behind him showed that he was being followed. Roane sighed. Who were they after, himself or Ragen? And he feared for that lady who had already started to wriggle her way into his heart.

Rouble looked around as he heard the door unlock and then lock to the office before he saw the two ladies. He was on his feet to hug both of them, surprising Ragen as he did so. He looked past them at Roane as he entered as well.

"What brings you two ladies here? I am sure that shopping was on your to-do list, Arin." He grinned at his daughter as she made a face at him.

"It is, Dad. Ragen needs work. You are behind in what you need to do and have stated that you need to hire a secretary. She hasn't done that but she's a quick learner, I can tell. It's working for you or working for Roane." Arin made a face at her brother as he shook a finger at her.

"Is that so? Ragen? What did you do for work?" Rourke turned his attention to that young lady.

"I worked in a medical lab. I don't want to go back to that. I'm too afraid to." Ragen wrapped her arms around herself in a defensive manner. "And I don't know what I would want to do."

"We'll look into that." Roane had approached her and just wrapped an arm around her, startling her with his action. "For now, Arin is correct. I do need

---

help as does Dad. It's your decision if you work for us or we can find someone who would hire you. That's is definitely not a problem. Here, there is good security and the police station is right next door." He grinned at Ragen as she frowned at him.

Ragen shrugged before she was walking through the building, seeing just what it was that Rourke did. She was amazed at the quantity of goods that were stored there. She paused, a finger out to touch a stuffed bear, blinking back the tears. Roane had followed her and stepped into wrap her once more into a hug. He felt the tears as they started and just held his lady and rocked slightly back and forth in a sideways manner to comfort her.

Rourke studied his son before he nodded. Roane was developing feelings already for that young lady, he could tell. He had reached out to a friend to investigate Ragen and would have to confess that to his son. Emma Finlay was not surprised to hear from him. She agreed to search through for what she could on Ragen and would be back in touch when she could. All Emma asked was if Roane and Ragen were safe at the present time. Rourke had acknowledged that for now they were. He just didn't know how long that would last.

Roane turned at last, swiping at his own face to wipe away the tears that he could not contain. He walked away for a moment to compose himself, seeing Arin moving in on Ragen and then leading her to the staff room. He sighed. This was not how today was to go. He needed to be in his office to work on other investigations that he had ongoing. He just didn't want to walk away from Ragen when she needed him. His hand reached for his keys before Roane walked outside and then stood and stared at his car before he drove away. He would find Ragen that night and talk with her, just to see what else he could find out that would help to move the investigation forward. Roane had spoken with Jerome who was at a loss at the moment as to why they had been kidnapped and just walked away or why John had been taken down as he had been.

Chapter 9

Ragen faced off against Roane that night, standing across his kitchen table from him. John stood nearby, still somewhat rocky on his feet, but with a grin on his face. He was certain that Ragen would win the face-off between the two.

"Ragen? John just wants to talk to you about your family. That's all." Roane was almost pleading with Ragen to talk with John. Only she didn't seem to want to do that.

"I can't, Roane. I just can't." A sob rose within Ragen as she turned and almost ran for the outdoors and then to the suite in the basement. She flung herself across her bed, the outside door locked behind her.

Roane stood for a moment, a hand in the air in a futile attempt to stop Ragen's flight before his head dropped. She was in flight mode, he decided, and needed time to come to terms with what she was remembering. And she was remembering, he could tell.

"Roane? It's okay. We'll talk tomorrow. Now, about you?" John studied his friend, not liking the stress and fear that was showing on Roane's face.

"Yeah, it is. Me? I don't know how to feel or what to think. Not any more." Roane turned to face John. "I have other investigations that I need to do. But this with Ragen? There's something off about it all that I don't understand."

"There is. Jerome is working it. I can't see it as I'm a victim as well." John was frustrated at that. "And I want to."

"And you can't even on your own time, can you?" Roane frowned at John. "Can they stop that?"

"They can't but I have to give any information to Jerome or one of the other detectives to verify. And I know that you are working it as you can." John grinned at his friend.

"I am as is my family. Dad said that he reached out to Emma for her input. And she will give that, we all know." Roane rubbed at his temple, a headache developing. "You need to go home, John, and rest. You're off for a few days yet?"

"I am, not that I want to be. I want whoever this was." John walked away, his eyes on the car parked across the street from Roane's house. He frowned for a moment before he nodded. Someone from one of the security teams that they knew was there, watching out for Roane and Ragen. That worked for now. Who knew how long it would take to work through all the paperwork and tips that seemed to be suddenly flooding the detective squad.

Ragen turned the next day, papers in her hands as she watched Roane work away. He really did need a secretary, she determined, but wasn't sure that was her. She sighed to herself. Ragen wanted to run and run as fast and as hard as she could. She had found a package on her doorstep that morning that she had not touched or moved. She had no idea what to do with it and that package frightened her.

Roane looked up at last, his pen stopping for a moment as he made notes on a case. He sat back in his chair before the pen was dropped to the desktop and he was on his feet to approach Ragen. He sighed to himself as she looked up in fear for a moment as she heard his footsteps.

"Ragen? How are you making out here?" He perched on the corner of the desk, his hand landing flat on the papers that she was moving around.

Ragen shrugged, her mind not really on her work. Her eyes sought those of Roane, frowning at the look in his eyes.

"Okay, I guess. You really do need a secretary." Ragen frowned at the desktop and the piles of papers that she had sorted and then filed into folders. "You need another filing cabinet, I think."

"I do. I have been lax in that." Roane was on his feet, his hand reaching for Ragen as he drew her to her feet, waiting as she grabbed at her purse before he had her out of the door and the security system set and the door locked. "We'll do that now and then head for the diner for lunch."

"We can't do that!" Ragen was shocked at his words, fastening her seatbelt before he drove away.

"We can and we will. We can call it a business lunch if you like." Roane stopped at his favourite diner, knowing full well that he never took any ladies out for lunch, other than his sisters or his mom or on occasion a cousin. "We can do this, Ragen. I just fear for your safety."

—

"Yeah, there's that." Ragen stared out of the side window, not willing to look at him. "I'll leave in the morning. Your safety matters too."

"I don't want you to walk away until we've solved this." Roane was around to open the door for her, a hand held out to help her from the car, a hand that he didn't drop as he walked towards the diner. Ragen stared at him and then at their hands. "And you will tell me about that package that you ignored this morning."

"I didn't open it, Roane. I just couldn't. I felt so much evil coming from it." Ragen bit at her lip, reliving her feelings from that morning. "Who found me? It had my full name on it."

"It did? I'll call Jerome and he'll get it and then speak with you once he's opened it." Roane was as good as his words, sending off a text to Jerome.

Jerome turned from Roane's front door. He had appeared, hoping to speak with either Roane or Ragen. He walked around to the door in the basement, staring down at the package.before he was taking photos of it and then stuffing it into a large evidence bag. He searched for anyone who might be around and found no one.

Heading for the crime lab, Jerome still hesitated about the package. He didn't like that it had appeared so suddenly or that Ragen's full name was on it. Someone was watching his friend too closely.

Roane looked up as Jerome approached him, standing and sliding onto the seat beside Ragen, watching his friend.

"What did you discover?" Ragen wasted no time in asking. She wanted whatever it was she was involved in over and over that day.

"An interesting assortment of items. Finish your meal and then we'll head into the department. I, for one, am determined to have my lunch today." Jerome nodded at the waitress as she placed his order in front of him and he bowed his head to ask a blessing on his food and then a plea for safety for Roane and Ragen.

Chapter 10

Roane stared down at the photos that Jerome had laid out on a table in a conference room at the police department. He frowned. There was something off about the contents of that package. His arm was around Ragen, helping her to stand. He could feel her body shaking from the strong emotions and fear that she was feeling.

"Ragen? Talk to us. Tell us about this." Jerome turned his head as he heard the door open and John appeared. He frowned at him for a moment before he nodded. John did need to be there. He was part of the investigation even though he was a victim of crime.

"I don't know. I have never seen anything like this before." Ragen refused to look up, her focus on the photos. "Who does this? These objects are bizarre. They mean nothing to me or my life." She looked up at last, her gaze focused on Jerome. "Can you tell me?"

"No, I can't, Ragen. I was hoping that you would know what these mean." Jerome's finger stabbed at each of the pictures. "Why would someone send you a parcel containing a blank journal, a calendar for the last year with every place you have been marked on it, a pen that was used to do just that, a picture of a house that you don't recognize, and this last? A staffed dog?"

Ragen was shaking her head by the time that Jerome finished speaking.

"I have no idea, Jerome. I truly don't." She spun and was running from the room, heading for the outdoors. The desk officer stopped her from leaving, a hand on her arm keeping her inside the building.

Jerome and the other two men strode after her, Jerome disturbed at her reaction. He felt sure that she was reacting to something in the photos but he couldn't be certain on that. Roane might have the best idea of what was going on but even he was a relatively new friend to the lady.

"Ragen?" Roane approached her, an arm around her, nodding at the officer as he moved back to his position at the desk. "Talk to me. Tell me what has you scared so badly."

Ragen sniffed, her emotions overcoming her for a moment. She simply shook her head. She had no idea what was going on or why someone would do what they had. All she could think of was that someone had been following her and following her too closely.

"Roane? You're an investigator. Would an investigator do that for a year?" She heard the indrawn breaths from both Jerome and John.

"They could. They would have to have been well paid but there are unscrupulous ones out there that would do what has happened." Roane led her back out to his car, tucking her inside and then sliding behind the wheel. "I think that you need to hear the story of my friends, Slavin and Shaye. And there are others who would gladly share what they have gone through. Some of them faced death from those who wanted to harm them."

Ragen nodded. She knew that from what Arin and Artis had told her, as well as from Sofi. She didn't want to face death but she knew that was a real possibility, given what she had been through.

"I want this over, Roane. How soon can we do that?" She refused to look at him, not wanting to see pity or any emotion like that on his face.

Roane nodded. Ragen wanted the same thing that he did. He had begun to treasure her as a friend and as a friend to her, he wanted her safe.

"We'll do our best. Unfortunately, we don't have a lot of information yet. We need to meet with our friends and see what we can come up. I know that my family will want to meet as well." Roane parked in his driveway, his eyes on his house. He was disturbed that someone had invaded his property in such a way.

Sofi turned from her stove late that afternoon, frowning at the sound of all the footsteps that she could hear. She moved to the kitchen doorway, seeing all of her family and Ragen as well as Slavin and Shaye and Nickol, another friend of the kids as she termed them. Sofi turned back to her kitchen, knowing that she had enough food for them all. A hug from John and then Jerome didn't surprise her. Both men were good friends with her family. Sofi looked past them and saw Peter, a security team leader, as well. She sighed. Their house had just been taken over by the kids and that meant they were planning on researching. Rourke stood for a moment before he hugged his wife.

"The kids are all here." He looked around, sensing someone close to them but not seeing anyone.

—

53

God was there, he decided, sending angels to protect his son and his lady. "We'll have enough food?"

"We do. I forgot for a moment that it was just us two. God led there, I suspect." Sofi turned to face her husband. "I am afraid, Rourke."

"So am I. God will protect the two, even though we may not like what they face. It is up to us to focus on finding the joy that they need in their lives and that joy can only come from God." Joy was a common theme in their discussions, reminding each other daily that joy came from God and they needed to find that emotion each day, drawing from God's promises to them.

Roane hesitated to approach his father after their meal and a time of prayer. He could hear the conversation coming from his father's office, laughter sprinkled among the words at times.

"Dad? How do we do this? How do we keep Ragen safe?" He had already described the package and the contents to everyone, Jerome and John remaining silent. They were there as friends that night, not as investigators, their supervisor aware of that..

"I don't know, son. She has seen something or heard something that she shouldn't have. What did she use to do?" Rourke had not gotten a good sense of Ragen's occupation.

"She worked in a medical lab. She told me that there had been concerns about contamination of some of the samples and possibly switching of other samples, but she had no proof of it. It was a rumour

---

that not one of the staff could confirm or deny." Roane was disturbed at that.

"I see. Well, let's see what we can determine. Emma has been in touch and sent some information that I haven't had a chance to look at." Rourke headed for his office, Roane trailing after him. His eyes found Ragen, sandwiched as she was between Shaye and Arin. He nodded. Those two ladies would take care of her, he knew, but that also placed them in danger. That made him fear for his family and their friends even more.

Chapter 11

Rourke studied the papers that he held, wondering how Emma had found the information that she had. He knew that Ragen was clutching her copy very tightly, so tightly that her fingers were white. Shaye had moved to let Roane sit in her place, finding Slavin waiting for her.

"Slavin? What is all this?" Shaye stared down at the papers as well.

"What is all this? This is Emma doing what she does best, finding the information that may well solve this." Slavin sighed. He knew this was far from over for his friends and that worried him to no end. He looked up, studying the soft green that the office walls were painted and then studying the photos that Sofi and Rourke had placed around the walls.

"I know that it is what she does. I just don't understand how she has connected Ragen to here. Ragen looked shocked when she read that." Shayne shifted to watch Ragen. "She's getting ready to run."

"I know but Roane will not let her. If she runs, he goes after her and brings her back. She'll not be able to hide from him for too long." Slavin's attention went back to the paperwork and he was lost in thought.

Roane's head tilted to watch his lady, his mouth opening to ask a question before he snapped it shut. Ragen wasn't ready to answer any questions yet, of that he was certain.

—

"Roane? I don't understand. How can I be related to this town? I was raised far away from here, on the other side of the province of Ontario in fact." Ragen was puzzled at that fact.

"I don't know, Ragen, but we'll look into that. I am sure that Emma has asked another friend to look at your family tree as well. Kat does that. Her husband is on Abe's security team. And Abe is Emma's husband." Roane's arm went around his lady, drawing her close to him and not finding her resisting him at all. Her attention was on the papers and the facts that Emma had found.

"How does she find this?" Ragen pointed to a name. "Who is this? I've never heard of this name. Yet, this Emma says he is related to me? And he's from this area?" She looked up in horror. "Is he the one who asked you to find me?"

Roane tilted her hand to read the name that she was pointing to. He knew the name, a man prominent in their town.

"He is from here and is prominent in town. I don't think that he was the one unless he disguised who he was. I did meet that man once in person." Roane sighed. "Of course, he could have had someone else meet me. And that is a real possibility."

"Would you know the man again if you saw him?" Nickol just had to ask that, his mind working overtime to try and understand what was happening. "I mean, he could have just been here for the day and that meeting and then left." He frowned at Slavin and Peter as they nodded in agreement.

—

"I don't know if I would." Roane's head went back as he groaned. "My security system. It should have a clip of him coming and going." His hand reached for his phone, pulling up his security system and then he was searching it, finding what he wanted. He handed his phone over to Jerome who frowned at him before his eyes dropped to the phot.

"This is not who he said he was. This man? He is known as an enforcer, both in and out of the drug trade. You were fortunate, Roane, that he just spoke with you and then left. That doesn't mean, however, that you are free of him. We need to find him and find him quickly. I am sure that he is following you and following Ragen." Jerome shared a look with John and then Peter. Both of those men understood only too well what could happen to the couple.

"I see. I have felt someone around but not all the time. It hasn't been as strong since I found Ragen. That would mean that he knows exactly where Ragen and I are all the time." Roane was on his feet and heading for the outdoors, needing to pace where there was room. Nickol and Slavin followed him, walking one on each side of their friend. "What do I do, guys? How do we keep Ragen safe? I don't like what Emma's found or what we just discovered." Roane stared around his parents' yard, not taking in the gardens and shade trees or the seating areas that his mother had arranged.

"That's a tough question, Roane. We don't have those answers for you. We have talked in the past to others who have been through these types of adventures, including Shaye and myself." Slavin dug his hands down into his jeans pockets, not sure how to respond. "All I can suggest is that you are aware of what and who is around you. Pray for protection. God does provide that for us in tangible and intangible ways."

"Slavin's correct. I have spoken in the past to those who have been through these types of adventures. Some of them are adamant that an angel protected them from real harm. God will only allow what is in His will for you. He is here with you. He has walked this path before you. He will never leave you at all." Nickol studied his friend before he drew in a deep breath. "You may not like what you face or what Ragen will face. You have already tasted what they can and will do to you."

"I know. It's hard not to be able to fully protect myself or to protect Ragen. She's not about to step back and let anyone do that. She has already told me that in a very forceful manner." A smile lit up Roane's face for a moment as he remembered the fierce look on her face as she tried her best to stare him down the day before as she uttered her words. "She will be out there. We can't stop her. All we can do is be there for her when we can. Ragen will not be smothered. That much I know. She'll hide how she's feeling. That comes from what she's faced her whole life." Roane turned as he heard a soft sound and watched Ragen walking towards him, walking into his hug and then not moving away from him. "Ragen? What happened? What did you find?"

Slavin reached for the paper that Ragen was clutching in her shaking hand. He studied her face,

—

shocked at the terror that was evident on it. He didn't know her well enough to know why she was so scared but something on that page had frightened her to that extent that her emotions were raw on her face.

"Ragen?" Roane waited somewhat impatiently for Ragen to respond. When she didn't, he gathered her into his arms and found a seat under the arbour in the centre of the yard, the other two men finding seats as well. His arms tightened around her as the men prayed for her. Roane raised his head, a frown in place as he gazed at Ragen, shocked to some degree at the terror she was evidencing.

"What's on that paper, Slavin?" Roane didn't look away from Ragen as he asked that question, knowing that the next words may well solve the problem of what she faced or else deepen the mystery. If he had been a betting man, he would have wagered that the contents on the page would deepen the mystery.

Chapter 12

Slavin studied the page in front of him, his lips mouthing out what he was reading. He paused in shock and almost horror at what he was reading. He had no idea who had found this.

"Who found this?" Slavin passed the paper to Nickol, sensing that someone had joined them. He turned his head slightly to see Rourke and Rowan beside them, with John standing outside of the arbour.

"Emma did." Rowan reached for the paper, almost not letting Nickol read it. "We had just received it from her, with a warning that someone needed to speak with Ragen first. We didn't get a chance to do that." His voice died away, leaving only the silence or what could be termed as silence from nature. They could all hear the birds singing away in a happy tune, the insects humming, the bees buzzing around the various flowers. A slight wind tossed at the tree branches and at their hair, moving in a warm wave of fresh air. The scent from the flowers hung heavy in the air. The sun played with the scudding clouds, peeking out for moments before being briefly covered by the white fluffiness.

"She did?" Rourke reached to take the paper, reading it. "Roane? Do you know Lou Walker?"

"Lou Walker? He's a private investigator but not from this area. I've seen him at conferences. Why?" He had not had a chance to read the paper. "What did Emma find?"

"What she found is not great for Walker. He's under investigation for stalking and for being part of a crime syndicate. Did you know that?" Rourke watched his son closely.

"No, I didn't." Roane's eyes closed as he groaned. "It was him that was following me the other day. I thought I recognized him but doubted myself as he is known not to leave his home area. Or is he?" He looked up at John, who nodded. "He's travelled the province and country, hasn't he, John? How many people has he destroyed?" Roane could not tamp down his anger, his arms tightening around the lady he held.

"You're correct on that. I can confirm that he is a person of interest in a case we're investigating. I can't say what case or why." John reached for the paper, reading it. "Emma will have forwarded on what she can for us. I'll leave this as I am only here as a friend today. If I need it, I'll ask for it with a warrant. That way nothing can be said when we go to court."

"And you think that we will?" Roane raised his head to stare at the sky. "How long will this go on for Ragen? She's right at the edge of breaking now."

Ragen shoved at Roane and sat upright, her eyes on the Rowan, who was nodding at her.

"Rowan? Is that true? Is that man after me?" Ragen's voice was barely audible.

"It is. Emma would not have stated that unless it was true. It's how she works. Everything that she sends on to either her client or the law enforcement people that need it is confirmed and she provides the confirmation. This goes for anyone who she has

---

working for her. And it is usually the person finding the information and confirming it that we speak with." Rowan knew that his words didn't relieve Ragen's fear or anxiety. "She'll keep working it, Ragen. If she needs to meet with you, she'll appear. And she will have her husband, Abe, with her or some of his security team. It's how they look after friends. Peter is friends with them as well as with two other security teams. If we need to move one of them in, we will. If we can speak with you before that happens, we do. If it is a case of your life or death and we don't have time, we move them in any way." Rowan watched Ragen as her face crumpled, a sad smile of sympathy on his face.

"It's too much, Rowan. I can't afford to pay her. And I know it's expensive. The same way that I can't afford to pay Roane. I need to leave and find somewhere to hide." Ragen sank back against Roane, not realizing that she had.

"Emma doesn't charge friends, and she will consider you a friend as you're friends with us. None of the security teams will do that either. And I know Roane will not charge you. In fact, he will likely pay you to work for him. If not, I have room for another secretary in my paralegal business. I work closely with Roane as does Dad and Ryley. We three are the paralegals in the family as well as keeping supplies for those who are in need and can't afford them." Rowan gave a quick grin as Ragen frowned at him.

"You would do that? You don't know me." Ragen yawned and then her eyes closed as she slept. She felt safe, she decided as she slept, something that she had not felt for a long time. How that was? Ragen

---

didn't know. She just knew that Roane made her feel that way, that he would protect in any way that he could.

Roane tilted his head to watch her, praying for her as he did so. Whatever she was facing was not over, and they really weren't all that much closer to knowing why.

"Do we even know why she was targeted?" Roane's voice was quiet as he spoke. He looked at his father as he asked that question, realizing that Peter and Jerome had appeared to join the group as had his mother. Sofi had found a seat next to her son, a hand resting on Ragen's back as she prayed silently for the couple. In her mind, they were a couple, whether they stayed that way or not. She could read her son enough to know that he was interested in getting to know Ragen better. Sofi just didn't know that lady enough to know how she felt. And Ragen kept her feelings closed, until today that was. Her terror could not be masked or hidden.

"Not really." John finally spoke. "We are looking into her background and that of her family. What we need from her, as you know, Roane, is a list of everyone, including anyone that she worked with." John walked away, disturbed at the threat on the letter from the man named Walker. Why he would do that, no one could tell John at the moment.

Late that evening, Ragen paced her apartment, trying to make sense of what she was going through. Jerome had reached out to her earlier, asking in an official manner for the names of her relatives, friends, and anyone who she had worked with. She had gladly given him that, already having created that document. Ragen stared around the kitchen, likely the colours that Roane had chosen. They were comforting, light greens and creams. She sighed. Ragen felt that she was getting too comfortable there and would hate to leave when the time came. The time would come, she decided, and soon. She couldn't continue to live there and keep Roane and his family in danger. Ragen didn't realize that was what the man after her wanted her to do - to leave the safety that she had found. He was unable to reach her, not yet. He had plans to do that but every time that he reached out to put them in place, he was stymied. That he didn't understand. He didn't understand that God was standing there and protecting Ragen and Roane.

Chapter 13

Growing as he hit the wall face first, Roane could feel the roughness of the brick scraping at his face and hands. He was unable to move, the men's hands shoving against his shoulders and back holding him there. Another groan came from him as fists pummelled at his back, hitting him in sharp hard blows. Roane didn't hear the words hissed at him in anger before the men were running away, their faces hidden by the upraised hoods.

Slumping to the ground, Roane waited for the men to return. His vision was blurred as his body lay in the debris that the wind had blown close to his brick encased building. He had come there that Saturday morning with the express intent of packing his office up and moving it to his home. He didn't feel safe in the downtown area any longer. This assault proved to be what he had feared.

A hand on his shoulder roused Roane somewhat but he couldn't answer the questions flowing at him. John crouched beside him, a hand on his friend, even as he called for assistance. On his feet, he paced around the building, not finding any evidence of what had happened. A gaze up to the security cameras drew another frown from him. They had been destroyed and a gaze at the nearby buildings showed the same. Someone had gone to a lot of work to hide this assault.

Back beside Roane, John watched closely as Roane was assessed and then loaded up to head for the hospital. His phone was out as he placed a call to

Rourke, one that he had dreaded to have to make, that another friend had been injured and the family was needed at the hospital.

Rourke had stared at Sofi in disbelief as he pocketed his phone.

"Roane was attacked at his building. John just called me." He reached to hug Sofi before he was turning them towards the door. "Where's Ragen?"

"With the girls and Shaye, I think." Sofi reached for her own phone, calling Artis. "Artis? Are you three with Ragen?"

"We are, Mom." Artis' steps slowed as she headed for a local book store. "Roane?"

"Yes, he's been hurt. John didn't give your Dad many details. But we need all three of you there. Yes, Ragen needs to be there." She pocketed her phone on Artis' questions.

Ragen had stopped beside Artis, her eyes on her new friend.

"Artis? It's Roane?" Ragen could barely get out the words.

"Yes. Mom said that John called and asked that we come to the hospital. He just said that Roane was hurt but didn't give a lot of details." Artis linked arms with her sister and Ragen doing what was asked of them as Shaye pointed towards her car. Shaye had driven the ladies downtown that Saturday morning. She was not willing to let the ladies go on their own. It was who she was.

Ragen's hands were clasped together as tightly as they could be as she waited with Roane's family, anticipation of how badly he was hurt colouring her thoughts. She didn't take in the colours of the waiting room, the gray tiled floor, the off white walls, or the coloured trim. Her focus was on the door to the examination rooms.

Rourke watched her closely, nodding as Artis and Arin sat on either side of her, their arms linked together. Roane was the first of his children to find his lady or guy, that he knew. The others were waiting on God's leading and he could see that happening with them as well even though none of them would acknowledge it.

John hesitated as he approached the cubicle where Roane lay, his eyes on the physician as he stood and stared at the computer screen, the images brought up for him to study.

"Doc? What can you tell me?" John's feet reluctantly took him forward to stand near the stretcher. He was concerned that Roane had not roused again, not from what he had been told.

"John? You're here? Of course you are. You want to know how he is." Doc Browne turned to study his young friend from church. "What is going on with Roane? He's never been here like this before and I understand that this is the second time that he has been assaulted in the last few weeks."

"That he has been. He's off on one of those adventure similar to what Slavin and Shaye had. His lady, Ragen, is with his family. She's not too sure

—

about Roane or any of us at this time." John was frustrated that he couldn't speak with Roane. He walked away, not wanting to, but knowing that he had to.

Rourke was on his feet, Sofi's hand tight in his as Doc Browne approached them. His heart sank at the grim look on the other man's face.

"Doc?" Rourke's voice was hoarse, his emotions evident in the tone of it.

"Rourke? Sofi? I'll take you back in a moment. For now, let's sit and I can let you and your family know what I can." Doc sank down gratefully into a chair, his eyes closing as he prayed for Roane and his family and yes, his lady.

"What can you tell us?" Rourke shifted his gaze between Sofi and the rest of his family, his eyes lingering on Ragen. That she was blaming herself was evident. "We know that Roane was heading to his office today with the thoughts of closing it up. His lease is almost up and he didn't want to continue working in the down town area."

"I wondered if he would. He's been restless the last little while, hasn't he?" Doc studied his close friend. "Roane was beaten once more. From what we can determine, he was shoved into the brick wall. The scrapes on his face and hands tell us that. As to the beating? We're still waiting for imaging to come back. Let's get you and Sofi back there for now and then the others can take turns." Doc was on his feet, heading back towards Roane, hearing the footsteps behind him. He didn't realize that Rourke had pulled Ragen to her

———

feet and with her hand tight in his and Sofi's tugged her with them towards Roane.

Ragen was shaking her head. She shouldn't be there. She wasn't a relative. Roane's siblings should be the ones coming back, not her.

"It's okay, Ragen." Sofi's soft voice stopped Ragen in her tracks for a moment. "Roane will want to know that you are safe. This way, you can see him and know that he's still alive." Sofi had watched Ragen over the time that they had been seated in the waiting room and had determined that Ragen was afraid that Roane was dead or else dying.

Chapter 14

Roane roused slowly in the early morning hours. He groaned as he tried to shift to his back, the pain not allowing him to do so. He stared around through partially opened eyes, not sure where he was. Jumping as he felt a hand on his shoulder, Roane's eyes closed once more before he opened them to stare up at Ryley.

"Ryley? Where am I and what happened?" Roane licked at his lips, his mouth dry. He nodded grateful as Ryley helped him to a sitting position on the side of the bed and then held the covered cup to that Roane could drink water through the straw.

"You were beaten, Roane, at your office. What happened?" Ryley waved his hands. "Forget that I asked. You have to talk to John or Jerome first. And yes, Ragen is fine. She's out in the waiting room with Artis and Rowan. She just wouldn't leave. She seems to think that you'll die or disappear on her." Ryley gave a smirk at his brother as Roane frowned at him. "And no, we're not springing you from here just yet. They want to repeat the ultrasound and x-rays in the morning. You're stuck until then."

"How bad?" Roane's head dropped until his chin rested on his chest.

"Bad enough that you won't be working for at least a week. Your kidneys are bruised. You have some bruised ribs. They beat you, Roane, while you were held against a wall. That's why your face and

—

hands are scraped." Ryley was more than a little concerned about his brother.

"I was? I don't remember. I can remember heading that way, intent on packing up the office." Roane groaned as he settled back on the bed. "What time is it any ways?"

"Three in the morning." Ryley turned as he heard soft footsteps, a hand coming out to draw Ragen closer to the bed. "He's awake, Ragen. He's not dying on you." Ryley stepped back as Ragen approached the bed, her hand covering her mouth to suppress her sobs.

Roane's arm came out to wrap around her as he struggled to sit once more. His eyes were on her face, seeing the stress and struggles that she was going through. This is hard, he thought. We need to find joy in life. This is sucking it from us big time. All Roane could do at the moment was hold Ragen and pray for her.

"You're okay, Roane?" Ragen could barely speak, her emotions were that strong. She has been so afraid that Roane was dying, despite the reassurances of his family.

"I'll be okay." Roane's finger traced a tear track on her cheek. "And what about you?"

Ragen shrugged, her eyes not raising to see him watching her closely.

Roane shared a look with Ryley who simply shook his head.

"It's Sunday, Roane. We'll move in and pack you up. You want your office stuff at home?" Ryley

---

had no doubt that they needed to get Roane out of that building.

"I do. The furniture can go in the garage. There's room. The filing cabinets and that paperwork and the computer can go into my office in the house." Roane sank back on the bed, his hand not letting go of Ragen's. His eyes closed as he slept, the pain driving him into a restlessness that was not relieved by the pain medication that dripped from the intravenous line into his hand.

"Will he be okay, Ryley?" Ragen tugged at her hand, not able to release it from Roane's grip.

"He will be. Ragen, he would do whatever he could to protect you. We don't know why he was attacked yesterday. It could be because of you. It could be because of one of his cases that he can't talk about." Ryley turned slightly as he heard other footsteps and his brother and sister stood beside him. "He would want you to stay safe. For now, that means staying with one of us or with our parents. Or we could go to a set of grandparents and let them look after you." Ryley gave a soft laugh at the snort from Rowan. "You know they'd do that, Rowan."

"I know. They would just lock the door and not let her out at all." Rowan moved to watch Ryley. "We've moving him today?"

"We are. Dad mentioned that last night. John and Jerome are off. Peter said his team would be around to keep watch and help. Slavin and Nickol are on board. Joseph said he'd bring in one of his moving trucks, a small one, to move him." Ryley shook his head. "I still don't understand it."

"None of us do. And I doubt that Roane will be able to help much. He was likely sucker punched at the beginning and didn't have any time to defend himself." Artis wrapped an arm around Ragen. "No one blames you, Ragen. You are a victim, juts like Roane. We don't understand why. But God has you both covered in the hollow of His hand. He is there with you always."

Ragen gave a brief nod. In her heart she knew that. It was in her head that she was having trouble accepting that. And that bothered her. She never had trouble trusting God. Right now, she was. She tried her best to choose joy in her life. And she just couldn't find joy in what she was going through and doubted that she would ever do that.

The next morning, Rourke turned from his son's office, locking the door behind him. The group of men had packed up Roane's office and the ladies had shown up to clean it. Ragen had stayed with Sofi who was doing her best to make Roane relax. That was a difficult task as he kept trying to find his shoes and go and help pack up his office. Ragen had finally resorted to shoving him into his office and then standing in the doorway, facing off against him. Roane was sore, hurting more than he could ever imagine he could hurt. He gave a brief smile at Ragen before he approached her and simply hugged her, surprising her at that.

"Roane? You need to rest. The guys will be here soon with your things. You've left instructions with your mother as to where you want what." Ragen was almost in tears as she shoved back from him. "Please? You can't heal unless you do relax."

Roane finally nodded, finding Ragen's hand and pulling her down on the sofa with him. His head went back against the sofa as his eyes closed. He slept, the pain medications taking over his desire to stay awake.

Ragen studied him and then studied the hands that were still clasped together. She tugged her hand free and was on her feet, heading to find Sofi, finding instead John who also hugged her. She was not used to this from new friends or any friends for that matter. Her mother had not hugged her, not that she could remember. And Ragen suddenly realized how bereft a childhood that she had had.

Chapter 15

Rowan turned from where he had set down Roane's desk chair. He was saddened that his brother had decided to give up his office but he could understand. Roane had been restless the last few months. When Rowan had approached him, his brother had just shrugged, not saying much other than he didn't know what was the matter.

Rourke's arm came to rest across his oldest son's shoulders. He was not sure what was going on with his family, other than his middle child was in danger but was also desperate to protect the lady in his life. Rourke knew that Roane would not willing walk away from Ragen. That much he could read in his son.

"What's Roane going to do, Dad? Work from here?" Rowan was puzzled by Roane's decision.

"For now, he will. He did ask your Mom and I to pray for him. He has been approached with a new opportunity but hasn't said much about it other than to ask for prayer. He said that he had asked all of you as well."

"He has, Dad." Rowan was equally puzzled by Roane's actions in this. "He knows that we don't need much information to pray for one another. I just think it's a life-changing decision."

"I have the same thought. For now, let's get him sorted out in the office. Ragen has taken on that task, directing all of us in where to put things. She's good for him. She is starting to speak up for herself."

—

Rourke locked the garage door behind them as they headed for the nearby house.

"She is." Rowan grinned as he recalled how Sofi had told them about how Ragen had made Roane relax.

"Now, Ragen? Are we all sorted out in here?" Rourke stood for a moment beside that lady, frowning at the look on her face. She looks lost, he decided, and the family needed to help her.

"I think so, as much as we can. Roane will need to go over it all and move what he wants to." Ragen's sober gaze was on that man as he slept, stretched out on the sofa. He had given in to her pleas to rest at last, not wanting to but also as a realist knowing that he had to. He had resisted the pleas of his whole family to do that. The family had just exchanged glances as he did what Ragen had begged him to rest.

Later that evening, Roane wandered his home, nodding at the neatness of the office. He opened his office filing cabinet, pleased that everything was back where it should be. He didn't hear Ryley behind him until his brother spoke. Roane jumped at that, before he spun. He sighed. He was jumping at everything and for good reason. Taking the cup of coffee extended to him, he sighed once more.

"Thanks, Ryley, for your help. I know. I know. We're family and that's what families do. Not all families do." Roane's eyes traced to the doorway. He knew that Ragen had left his home and was in the suite downstairs. That was not where he wanted her. Roane wanted Ragen at his side. He didn't understand that emotion, not realizing how much she was working her way into his heart.

"It is. And I know that Ragen was watching us closely today. We need to make her a permanent part of the family. And that's what you do, Roane. I can see you watching her and she is watching you too." Ryley looked around the office. "You're okay working here for now?"

"I am. I don't know how much longer I'll do this work. It has been all I wanted to do as a teenager and young adult. Now? I guess I've seen too much and been asked to cross the line too many times." Roane didn't see Ryley's reaction.

"Roane?" Ryley waited patiently for Roane to turn and face him, When he didn't Ryley moved to stand in front of him. "Roane? What did you just say?"

Roane stared at his brother, not sure what Ryley was asking.

"I don't understand what you're asking, Ryley/"

"You said that you have been asked to cross the line many times. Do you have the names of those who asked that?" Ryley once more waited patiently, his eyes raising to where Arin stood in the doorway.

"I said that? I guess I did. I was just thinking out loud. I do have a list but I'm not getting it out tonight. Tonight? I need to rest. Now, we need to have a meal. Arin?" Roane had turned to see his sister watching him. "Ragen?"

"She's sleeping, Roane. She let me have a key to the apartment." Arin was blinking back tears, her emotions raw for a moment. "Do you understand how much that cost her to trust us that much?"

"I do, Arin." Roane moved to hug his sister before he walked past her and to the outdoors. He found his favourite seat on the back porch and sat, his eyes on the darkening sky. This was the time of day that he spent time with his Creator in silence.

Ryley had followed his brother, stopping at the back door. He didn't need to follow his brother to know that he was hurting more than just physically.

"Ryley? Was he serious?" Arin wrapped her arm around her brother's, her head leaning against it.

"He was. I should have asked him earlier. There just hasn't been enough information coming at us to determine what or who." Ryley sighed as his phone chimed. He pulled it out to read the text message. "Emma and Abe are heading this way tomorrow. They have asked if Peter would be available."

"She's found something then. I would guess that she's also talked to Don and Richard to get their feelings or else Abe has." Arin moved to where she had a meal in the crockpot, reaching to dish out the stew.

"I would suspect so. And that means there much be a great deal of danger for both Roane and Ragen." Ryley took the bowls and set them on the table, heading outdoors to find his brother. "Roane? Arin has our meal on the table. Let's eat and then we can spend some time in prayer."

—

"Thanks, Ryley." On his feet, Roane found his sister, giving her a hug as he thanked her. Their family was larger and noisy at times but he didn't know that they had ever really had a falling out. They had been taught from when they were young to pray through what they were struggling with and with the person who they needed to do that.

Chapter 16

Two weeks later, Ragen paced the back yard, not seeing Roane standing and watching her and then watching the area around them. She was frustrated and afraid, if those two emotions could be said to be felt together. She turned and found Roane just feet from her. Ragen was afraid for him, not sure why, but knowing that their lives had become entwined when Roane was asked to find her. That was something they were working through but not getting too far in identifying the person responsible for that request. Any information that Roane had had on that person had disappeared from the internet and his email.

"Roane? Where do we go from here?" Ragen refused to move closer to him, suddenly deeply afraid for the tall handsome man who was becoming important to her.

"We continue to work through what we have. Emma has had to set it aside for now due to urgent requests for information. She hasn't wanted to but it is what can happen." Roane sighed deeply, his eyes on the houses around them. He felt watched and didn't know why. Someone was in a neighbouring house and keeping track of what he and Ragen were up to.

"I get that, Roane. I'm just so afraid today. And I don't know why." Ragen approached him, accepting the hug that he offered. She had not been a hugger until she met his family. Now, their typical greeting was a hug.

———

"I know that you are. So am I. God is here in this situation with us, even when it seems so dark and frightening. He has us wrapped in His protection and care." Roane turned them to walk back towards the house. "We've managed to get caught up on everything for the day. I am waiting for information to come back. How be we find something fun to do?"

"Fun to do? Roane!" Ragen shook her head. She just wasn't sure about this man and what he could mean to her future. She had been working for him on a part-time basis and for his father the rest of the week.

"We need to focus on something else for a few hours, Ragen. If we don't, the burden of fear and worry will wear us down. And that is what they want. If we are worn down, we are not as alert as we should be. And I don't want you to disappear on me. Ever." Roane wasn't watching her face and didn't see the look of hope and wonder that coloured it.

"Roane? Do you mean that?" Ragen stopped walking, bringing Roane to a halt as well.

"Did I mean what? What did I say?" Roane couldn't exactly remember his words. All he could hear was the sounds of nature around them.

"That you don't want me to disappear." Ragen was frustrated that he didn't seem to remember what he had said.

Roane turned to face her, studying her face before he nodded. She was the lady of his dreams, he decided.

"I do, Ragen. I really do. I want to date you but I don't know if you are ready for that." Roane hugged her and then just stood, his arms around her in a loose manner.

"You do? I'm dangerous." She poked at his chest with a slim forefinger as he laughed at that. "I am. And so are you. Did you ever find out anything about the men who wanted you to become involved in crime?"

"Jerome had someone investigating that. He sent me a message this morning that they were arranging arrest and search warrants on a couple of them. He simply asked that I take care and keep as safe as I could."

"And that is difficult." Ragen leaned against Roane for a moment. "How do we investigate this?"

"My family and friends want to meet on Saturday once more. Dad has some information that he is confirming that he wants to go over with us all. He said that it is wider and deeper in scope than he expected it to be." Roane reached to lock his back door before taking Ragen's hand and walking around to the front of the house. His steps slowed as he saw the two men waiting for him, a frown on his face. "Richard? Don? You two are here? I don't think that I like this."

Richard grinned for a moment even as Don gave a short laugh. They had security teams who had gone through adventures with their now spouses. Long-time friends, the men had been approached by Emma to meet with Roane and Ragen. Peter was walking rapidly towards them, called in by Emma as well.

—

"We need to meet with you two but you were heading somewhere." Richard waited for Roane to speak.

"We were. We were heading out for a meal." Roane looked past the three men to see one of the servers from his favourite diner approaching him. "Todd?"

Todd grinned, holding up a large plastic bag.

"Sara sent me. Don't ask me how she knew there were three extras. You know that she can't tell us that." Todd handed over the meals and then ran for his car.

The five shared a look before the men shook their heads. This was not unheard of in their towns. Ragen just didn't know what to think.

Finishing their meal, Richard helped to gather up the debris, his eyes shifting between Roane and Ragen. It was becoming more dangerous for them. There was evidence that they were being closely watched. Roane had admitted that he was searching every day for unwanted surveillance equipment and also searching his car for trackers. So far, he had not found anything but they all knew that could change, depending on how close the men were able to get to them.

"Ragen? Talk to us. Tell us about your life." Richard reached for a pad of paper and his pen.

"What can I tell you that I haven't before? I've given everything that I can think of. All my relatives and friends. I just don't know what more I can say." Ragen was frustrated at Richard's request, not able to understand that going back over everything again and again would open up the information that was needed.

"It's what we do, Ragen." Don spoke up, his eyes rising to the doorway where Rourke and Sofi now stood. "Your parents are here, Roane. Let's spend some time in prayer before we go back to what we were asking. We need to bathe you two in prayer. This is where it becomes more dangerous for you both, not knowing who is after you. You're looking over your shoulders all the time, suspecting everyone around you including your friends."

Chapter 17

Ragen rose at last, walking away from the kitchen to stand in Roane's office. She was frowning, trying to come to terms that someone in her past wanted to harm her. The consensus had been that whoever had asked Roane to find her had not done so for her good or health.

Sofi had followed the lady who had become important in their family. They had opened up the family and just absorbed her into it as Rowan had said. They all knew that she was important to Roane.

"Ragen? What's troubling you?" Sofi's soft voice brought Ragen's attention to the lady that she was beginning to think of as a mother.

"I don't know. I don't know enough about my family to understand why they acted like they did. They never seemed to want me. Anything I received was done grudgingly." Ragen drew in a deep breath, troubled by her thoughts. "How do I know if they are really my parents? I always wondered that. I don't look like any of them."

Sofi reached to hold Ragen as her emotions overwhelmed her. Rourke and she had talked it all over that morning and that was what they had asked each other. Rourke had reached out to Emma and asked that. Emma had replied that fact had been raised by one of her team that morning and that team member was working through that. He hoped to have some information on that fact later that day.

—

"Rourke and I have wondered that. Emma has a team member looking into that. She'll confirm it either way. For now? What can we do for you?" Sofi drew her down to the sofa, her arm still around her, praying aloud for the younger lady.

"I don't know." Ragen sniffed as she tried to control her tears. "I don't cry, you know."

"It is understandable that you are now. Tears can help us cope. God gave them to us for a reason. And He does bottle our tears. They are that important to Him."

Ragen nodded. She had understood that for years but had never experienced it for herself. Now she had. She breathed a prayer of thanks to her Abba Father.

"How do I do this? I need to stay safe. And I need to keep Roane safe." Ragen sighed. "He told me this morning that he wants to date me."

"He did? He will have prayed through it all, including the danger that you are both in. You are important to him, Ragen. He has never reacted to a young lady as he is with you. There has been interest on the young ladies' part in the church. He has just moved through life as a single man. Until now. If he has asked that, then he is looking forward to the future. That future includes you in his mind."

"He hasn't?" Ragen looked surprised at that. "That's unusual, isn't it?"

"Not that unusual. We have a number of men as friends or who we know who are like that. It's how

—

87

they were led to live their lives." Sofi grew silent, allowing Ragen time to understand what she had stated. "Our sons are like that. Rowan and Ryley have found their ladies and Artis and Arin have found their fellows. Roane has been waiting for you."

Ragen was silent, trying to understand what was being said to her. She blinked for a moment, seeing Roane leaning against the door frame to the living room, his feelings for her open on his face. She was on her feet, moving into his space, accepting that he was important to her as well.

"Ragen?" Roane's voice was low. "We'll talk. For now, Peter has a question for you. Can you come back and talk with us?" He waited patiently for her to respond, knowing that he would wait for as long as it took for her to do that.

"I can." Ragen hugged Roane and then moved past him, her trust level for him and his family and friends rising. She had had trouble trusting people all of her life, without knowing why. Roane was changing that.

Later that afternoon, Roane stared down at his notes. They had made some progress, he thought, but everything just seemed too muddled for him to get straight at the moment. He rose from his kitchen table and stepped outside, standing in the cooling air of coming night, drawing in a deep breath. Roane had no idea where this was all heading but it was heading somewhere. And that somewhere scared him. He was afraid for Ragen, himself, and then his family. The sense that Don had mentioned was that whoever it was could well go after his family to get to him. As to why

—

that was no one yet had a good sense. Ideas had been tossed around and noted down but none seemed to make sense.

Ragen stood for a moment, her eyes on Roane before she moved towards him, ducking under the arm that he raised to wrap around her.

"Roane? Did we accomplish anything today?" Ragen wasn't sure on that.

"We did. We have ideas and notes that we need to work through. Tomorrow, I need to work on what I have outstanding. You're with Dad, right?" At her nod, Roane drew in a breath of relief. There was good security at his father's office, much needed. A frown crossed his face for a moment.

"Roane? What if what we're going through isn't directed at you or even me? What has your Dad been involved in that would merit something threatening his family?" Ragen spoke the words that Roane had not wanted to.

"That's a good question, sweetheart. And I'll talk with Dad when I drop you off in the morning. I know that you have a driver's license and need a vehicle. For now, how be we let that rest? You could be out on your own and disappear without us knowing for a long time. We might never find you. I can't handle that thought." Roane rested his chin on her hair, content for the moment.

"That's what I wanted to speak with you about but just didn't know how to. I do drive but haven't for a few months. I agree with your thoughts but driving me around puts you and whoever it is at risk, doesn't it?"

"It does but it's a risk we're willing to take for you. Artis and Arin are in agreement with that. They can protect themselves in most circumstances. I have a friend who teaches self defence. He approached me to ask if you wanted to take lesions free of charge from him. He's worried about you." Roane waited patiently for her to think through his words. That was something he understood about her. She needed time to think through what was said to her and then respond.

"I would like that. I have some training but had to give it up when I left home. I have missed that." Ragen stepped away from Roane. "I'm retiring, Roane. Today was stressful and I am exhausted."

Chapter 18

Three days later, Ragen walked rapidly around the house to her apartment door, opening it and then locking it behind her. She dropped the handful of mail onto the kitchen table before she headed to change out of her more dressy clothes that she wore to the paralegal office. Rowan had been her escort that afternoon, waiting patiently as she headed for the mail box and then walking her around to her door. He had then walked the yard and around the house and garage, searching for anything out of the ordinary and not finding it. Rowan knew full well that Roane was doing that but the men in the family had decided among themselves that they were search as well, just as an added level of security for the couple.

Grabbing the mail, Ragen headed for Roane's place, finding the back door unlocked as it was always for her at that time of day if she wasn't working with him. She stopped in his kitchen, eyeing the crockpot on the counter. Sofi had simply stated that she had left a meal for the pair and they were to make sure that they ate. A soft smile covered her face. Sofi was taking care of her just like a normal mother would do. She had never had that.

Roane lifted his head for a moment, a smile crossing his face. Ragen were here and safe. That had been his prayer over the day. He had grown increasingly worried over the day and could only pray for his lady. He had too much work on his desk that he needed to get to. Roane's eyes went back to his computer monitor as he typed rapidly to finish off the report that he had promised that day. Finishing it, he rapidly read back through it. Satisfied, he sent it on to his client through his secure email and then closed down his work for the day. On his feet, he walked rapidly towards the kitchen, pausing for a moment to watch Ragen as she moved around that room, dishing up their supper and then turning as she felt his presence.

Roane was across the kitchen, wrapping her into a hug and then praying for her. Ragen's head rested against him. She was getting used to this sort of greeting from him at the end of the day and had to admit to herself that she was liking it.

"Have a good day, sweetheart?" Roane reluctantly let her go and reached to pour their water into glasses that he set at their places at the table.

"I did. Your father is so good to work for. And their work is so interesting." Ragen sat and then waited as Roane reached for her hand to ask a blessing on their meal. "How about you?"

"I did. I was able to get through all that I had to do and sent off what reports were promised for today." Roane studied the pile of mail. "You grabbed the mail?"

"I did. I haven't had a chance to sort through it. That can wait until tomorrow. It's usually just work mail for you." Ragen frowned at the sense of danger that suddenly washed over her. "At least that's what I think."

"We'll look at if later. For now, what are your plans for tomorrow? It's Saturday." Roane grinned at her as her frown turned towards him.

"I don't know. Some fellow seems to think that he needs my time on a Saturday. Any idea who that might be?" A sparkle in her eye belied the sternness of her words.

"I have no idea. But will you spend the day with me?" Roane's hand rested on hers, stilling the restless movements of her. "I have a question, Ragen. Did you have an apartment that needs to be cleaned out?"

Ragen shook her head. It wasn't the first time that she had been asked that question and every other time she had refused to answer, not sure why she was being asked that. Her trust level of people trying to help her had been low. Roane and his family had changed that for her, as had his friends who were becoming her friends.

"No, I don't. I had quit my work and at that time, I gave up my apartment. I knew that I could find work anywhere in the province with my qualifications." Ragen sighed. "I didn't expect to have you find me that day. And I still don't understand who asked you that."

"I don't either. That contact information has disappeared. Even Emma can't find it and that is unusual." Roane sat for a moment, his fork poised over his plate of food. "And that worries us all. If we don't know who asked me to do that, we can't protect you."

"You can't do God's job for Him, Roane. He is in control and has walked this path before us. He is here with us. He will protect us, allowing only what is in His will for us." Ragen stared down at her plate, losing her appetite as she spoke. She shoved the plate away from her. "I want this over, Roane, but I don't know that it will be over very soon. You state that you don't have the information that you need. We're both looking over our shoulders when we're out and about. I have companions with me when I'm out on my own. If I don't see them, I can still sense that they are there."

"They are, sweetheart. They are. My friends are worried about you. John and Jerome have arranged for off-duty officers to protect you." His hand went up to still her words. "It's what we do in our town. We look after our friends. And you are a friend to us."

"And I appreciate that. But they can't do it for the long term. Whoever it is has shown that they don't care if we have security. They just wait until we're on our own. And that will happen sooner or later. It always does. I've talked to some of your friends' wives and understand what can happen." Ragen sighed, her face dropping into her hands. "I want this over, Roane. How do we force whoever it is to show their hand?"

Roane had listened intently to her words, hearing the plea behind it to have it all over with. That wasn't happening at the moment. They just didn't have that information that was needed.

"I get what you're saying, Ragen. How be tomorrow we take a look at what we have? Abe and Emma would like to meet with us if that's possible." Roane waited for Ragen to respond, letting her have that control over what she did.

—

"I think that we need to." Ragen grinned at him suddenly. "How many are going to be here?"

"My family. Slavin and Shaye. Nickol. I don't know if John is available. Peter would come if we asked." Roane waited once more for Ragen to respond. He drew in a deep breath when she didn't.

Ragen studied her hands. This was affecting too many people, she decided.

"I want to go on the offensive, Roane. How do we do that?" Ragen rose and walked away, the back door closing behind her.

Chapter 19

The next morning, Ragen stared down at the addressed envelope that lay on the desk in front of her. She had sorted out the mail, setting aside the business mail and then handing Roane his personal mail. He had moved away to open that mail, not seeing the fear that now covered Ragen's face. She continued to stare at the envelope. It was addressed to her at Roane's address. She knew of no one other than his family and friends who knew where she was. Her friends had been left in the dust, so to say, and she had no contact with them. And she had no contact with her family.

Peter and John had entered the office at that point and stopped abruptly. John moved to stand beside Ragen even as Peter headed outside to search for anything that didn't belong.

"Ragen?" John's voice beside her caused Ragen to jump before she stared at him. "What's wrong with that letter?"

"What's wrong with it? It's addressed to me. With this address. Who did this?" Ragen backed away, hitting Roane who had raised his head at the way her voice kept rising as she spoke and had walked to stand nearby. His arms went around her and steadied her on her feet.

"Ragen?" His voice was low in her ear.

Ragen just continued to shake, her fear driving that. She just pointed at the desk, not moving that way at all.

—

"John?" Roane then turned his attention to his friend, not seeing the comfortable office that he had created.

"Roane? Ragen received this letter. Do you have a pair of latex gloves and a plastic bag or two?" John reached for the desk drawer that Roane had merely pointed towards. "Let's see what this says."

John carefully opened the envelope, not sure what was inside of it. He dumped out the contents and then reached for the letter, unfolding it to read it. John frowned. He turned to Ragen, finding her frowning at him in deep concentration. He then looked at the photos that had fallen to the desk. John sighed to himself. He had come as a friend that day. The envelope and its contents had changed that.

"John? What does the letter say?" Roane shuffled Ragen forward despite her attempts to resist that.

"The letter? It's garbled from what I can see. It's not making sense at all." John had bagged the letter and now laid it flat on the desk. He nodded at Roane reached for his camera to take a photo of it. "Ragen? Do you know a Theodore Thomas?"

Ragen shook her head. That name was unknown to her.

"I don't. Who is he?"

"He has signed the letter." John looked over as Roane made a sound. "Roane?"

"He's a private investigator for a nearby town. Why would he be writing to Ragen?" Roane was puzzled at that, He knew the man and had met him on a number of occasions. He just didn't like him and had no reason for that.

"That what we need to find out. The photos? He's been following Ragen over the years by the looks of it." John was afraid for the lady who meant so much to his friend. "Why would he be doing that?"

"You'll have to ask him that." Ragen studied the photos. "Not over the years. Just the last six months. He's followed me as I went about my daily walk, including after I resigned my position and left. He just doesn't seem to have found me in Toronto."

"No, there are no photos from there. Either that was done deliberately or you were able to hide well enough from him." John turned to Roane. "How did you track her down?"

Roane shrugged. He couldn't rightly state how he had. He had prayed about finding her and felt the strong nudge from God to head for the Toronto bus station that day when he found her.

"I just followed God's leading. I can't explain it other than that way." Roane's head dropped for a moment. "And someone who has never done that will never understand."

"We do understand that, Roane." John reached to bag the photos. "I'm heading in with these to give to the lab. I'll be back, I think." He walked away, nodding at Peter as he did so. He knew that his cousin would stay around for now, just to protect their friends.

―

"Roane? Who did this?" Ragen was pacing, uncertainty in her movements.

"I don't know, Ragen. I wish that I did. I would face off with them and stop them." Roane's anger was growing and he knew that would not help. He just had to vent and he would not do that in front of Ragen. Roane turned as he heard footsteps and his family appeared. "Good. You're here. Take a look at these photos." He pointed to his computer. He had managed to upload the photos to that machine.

"What are these, Roane?" Rowan frowned as he watched the photos flicking across the monitor screen.

Ragen turned on him, her rage at the event evident to the puzzled family.

"Some private investigator was following me for months. Those are what those photos are." Her finger stabbed towards the screen. "The only place he didn't seem to find me was in Toronto. Roane knows him." Ragen turned and almost ran from the room, Ryley on her heels, not wanting her to be on her own.

"Ragen? Don't run. That's what they want you to do. If you run, you'll disappear. We may never be able to find you." Ryley's hand on the back door prevented Ragen from opening it.

"I have to, Ryley. I can't stay here. I am putting you all in danger if I do." Ragen's sobs broke Ryley's heart, knowing that Roane would not let her walk away from him. If she did, he would be right after her.

"No, we don't know that for sure. We don't have a good sense yet on why this is happening." His hand

—

99

went up to stop her words. "Yes, Roane has been assaulted and is still recovering. We don't know that he was targeted because of you. That's not clear. It could be one of his cases that caused it. Or it could be a case that one of us is working on with Dad. They may have gone after Roane to try and make us quit."

Ragen stared at him, her eyes huge. She had heard those words before but today, Ryley's words had gotten through to her.

"It could be? Yes, it could be. Let's find out what we can." Ragen turned, coming to a halt at the appearance of a couple a few years older than herself. She didn't know them but obviously Ryley did by the way he greeted them.

"Ragen? This is Abe and Emma Finlay. They are to meet with us, I gather from what Roane had said."

"They were." Ragen stalked towards Emma, standing in front of her. "Can you solve this today?"

Emma grinned at her even as Abe gave a soft laugh before she reached to hug the other lady.

"We'll do our best but there is still information coming in that needs to be verified. How be we find your fellow and spend some time in prayer?" Emma watched Ragen closely, seeing the stress that she was under.

Chapter 20

Emma watched Ragen carefully over the day, a frown sometimes in place. She was certain that she knew Ragen but for the moment set that thought aside. Where she knew her from would come to her, Emma thought, and then sighed. Ragen had been in their town of Riverville within the last two months and Emma had met her at their church. She didn't know if Ragen would remember her or not.

"Ragen? We've met before." Emma sat beside Ragen, startling her with her words.

"We have? I don't remember you. Where did we meet?" Ragen's attention was on Emma, not feeling Roane sitting down beside her.

"At our church. That was within the last two months. How long were you on the run?" Emma's hand reached for the pad of paper and pen that Abe was handing to her. His attention was on Ragen as well.

"It was? I moved around so much that I lost track of where I was." Ragen was on her feet, her hand reaching for the photos before she sat back down. "Please. Go through this and tell me where the towns are if you can."

Emma nodded as she took the photos, her eyes on Ragen for a moment. She's ready to run, Emma thought. If she runs, Roane goes after her. That's when it becomes so dangerous for them.

"Don't run, Ragen." Abe spoke up, bringing Ragen's attention to him. "It never works if the person in danger runs. We can't help to keep you safe if you do."

"I know that, Abe. It's how all of us feel, isn't it?" Ragen sank back against Roane without realizing that was what she was doing.

"We do. Emma and I did escape for a few days to find the eagles that she has been following. That placed us in more danger as the men after us found us. We also didn't tell anyone where we were going. That meant we could have disappeared and never been found. Don't do that to yourself or anyone else." Abe was on his feet, his phone out as he took a call from his business partner and good friend, Murphy. He stood where he could watch Roane and Ragen, seeing the stress that they were under but also the interest in one another that they were trying hard to hide from everyone else. That wasn't working out that well, he decided.

"These are interesting, Ragen. You've been tracked from Northern Ontario, do you know that? The last photo was in Elmton." Emma looked up as Ragen gave a small sound. "Ragen?"

"How did I not know that I was being followed? I was moving rapidly, I know, just running from what my life had been. I think I was hoping and praying to find a town where I could be safe and make a new life for myself. All I have is what was in my backpack. Until now. Sofi, Artis, and Arin are changing that for me." Ragen grew more sober than she had been. "Roane knows who took the photos. That man sent a letter that doesn't make sense."

Emma took the copy of the letter that she was handed by Sofi with a soft thank you. She studied it before she had her phone out to take a photo of it and then to send that copy on to one of her staff.

"My staff will work on this. They will also research this man." Emma looked around Ragen at Roane. "You know him, Roane?"

"I have met him. He's a private investigator from a nearby town. John took the originals of everything, which is fine with us." Roane drew in a deep breath. "How do we prove this man is involved other than as an investigator?"

"We will investigate him thoroughly. To tell you the truth, his name did come up and we are researching him for someone else. Your name has come up in that investigation. I need to confirm more information and then we will talk about that." Emma was on her feet, her phone out to take a call.

Ragen watched her walk away, feeling as if a lifeline that had been thrown out to her had just been withdrawn. A small whimper of fear came from her.

Roane just wrapped her into his arms, his chin resting on the top of her head. All he could do was pray for her and stay as close to her as she would allow. That was something that he was working on, having to leave it in God's hands despite how much he wanted to be the one protecting her all day and all night.

Ragen paced around the house, needing to be outside. She knew that someone was beside her. Just which of the men it was, she didn't know, but she felt safe for the moment. Ragen's eyes were clouded with tears and she swiped at the ones that were falling. A handkerchief appeared in her line of sight and she took it with a soft thank you.

Luke, one of Abe's team members, walked beside Ragen. He had volunteered to travel with Abe and Emma that day, leaving the other six on their team working on Roane's and Ragen's adventure. They were making progress, he knew from the updates that the trio were receiving. But there was still a long way to go. And that frightened Luke. He knew only too well from his own adventure and those of his friends just how dangerous it was for the couple.

"Ragen?" Luke's voice finally broke through the fog that she felt she was in. "I'm Luke, one of Abe's team. What can I do for you?"

"What can you do for me?" Ragen stopped, her eyes on Luke's face. "Why would you ask me that?"

"Because it's what you need to hear. You need to hear that you are not alone. I know that your faith is being tested, that you doubt God is with you and will protect you. You want to fight this through on your own. That never works. Why did I ask that? Because you need tangible help, to know that someone is in your corner and is working to solve whatever this mystery is. You know that in your heart but sometimes our minds play tricks on us and causes us to doubt those around us."

"You've put my thoughts into words, Luke. Thank you." Ragen began to walk again, Luke at her side. "You all went through stuff, didn't you?" She saw Luke nod. "Okay. So, what would you do?"

"What would I do? I wouldn't hide. It never works, just delays the ending of the adventure. I don't mean that you put yourself out there right now. That may. have to happen but for now? Go about your daily walk. Have someone with you when you can. Be aware of what and who is around you. Don't be afraid to ask for help. Most importantly? Pray for strength, for courage, for answers, and for God's protection."

"Thank you, Luke. You have been a source of encouragement for me." Ragen turned to find Roane watching her and walked back towards him and into his hug.

Chapter 21

The next afternoon, Roane rose from his office chair, a frown on his face. He had been reading through the email that Emma had just sent him. The contents were disturbing. He didn't understand how she had found the information on that PI but she had. Now, Roane had to digest what she was saying and then decide how to react to it.

Ragen looked around from where she was seated on the front porch, curled up as she was in a brown wicker chair, a bottle of water held in her hand. She had been bored, not knowing what to do, and had just decided to spend time with her Abba Father outdoors in His creation.

"Roane? What did you discover?" Ragen watched him closely as he sat in the chair near her.

"What did I find? Emma sent on information on that investigator. I know. I know. It's Sunday and we made an agreement to leave it for today. I couldn't, sweetheart. We'll go over it in a bit. For now? What were you up to?" Roane grinned at her for a moment, his feelings for her open on his face without him realizing that they were.

"What was I up to? Not much. I'm bored, Roane. And I need to do something to combat that. What do you suggest I do?" Ragen's words were bit out, her anger evident. It was not directed at Roane but at the circumstances in which she found herself. Being on the run and hiding out had not been plans for her life that she had ever considered until now. And she hated those feelings.

"You do need to do something to combat that. We didn't get our day out yesterday. You're to work with me tomorrow. I'm closing the office and we're going to do something fun. I need a break just as you do." Roane shook his head as Ragen opened her mouth to protest. "It's okay, sweetheart. It's okay. I take days like this every couple of months. I have to. It helps to clear my head and keep me thinking clearly. Setting aside work for a day doesn't hurt. Even God rested on the seventh day. He knows that we need to come aside every once in a while. This is my way of doing that."

"Okay. So, this day out? Where were you thinking?" Ragen was challenging him, and they both knew that.

"Where would you like to go?" Roane could make that decision and knew that Ragen would just go along with him. "You need to take control of your life back. This is one way for you to do that, by making a decision as to what you want to do. I'm fine with that."

"I know you are. I just don't know where to go." Ragen's arms wrapped around her knees as her cheek rested on them. Her eyes never left Roane's face. "You have friends all over. Who would you want to visit?"

"Who would I want to visit? Let me think about that. We are close to many of them. How be we head to Elmton? Richard, who was here the other day, lives there. He would be willing to spend some time with us as would his team. There are also others there, including the pastor and his wife, who would talk with us.”

“That many?” Ragen drew in a deep breath. “Okay, Elmton is it. It’s not that far, is it?”

“Not really. Only about a thirty minute drive. Or we could head the other way and find Emma and Abe. But I don’t think that’s what you want.” Roane was certain of of words.

“No, I don’t think so.” Ragen drew in a deep breath. “This is hard, you know.” She looked around, certain someone was with them but not seeing anyone. “Have you ever been to the town of Mistletoe?”

“I have, many times. I have friends there who are descendants of the original founding families. They had quite the adventure.” Roane nodded. “So, instead of Elmton, we head for Mistletoe. Again, it’s not that far a drive.”

“No, it’s not. But I’m scared, Roane. What if something happens on the way there or back?” Ragen was sober as she spoke.

“It could happen anywhere. We can’t live in fear. I don’t want that for you or for me. We weigh the risks and then make the decision on what we want to do.” Roane reached for her hand, his head bowing as he prayed for his lady and then himself.

Ragen stared ahead of her, watching the light traffic that moved through the streets, the occasional walker with their dogs, and then looked up. She was conflicted, she knew, wanting to choose joy in her life but too afraid of what might happen to her or Roane and his family. There was no evidence to suggest or determine just who the person was after.

Roane waited patiently for Ragen to respond to him. When she didn't, he sighed to himself. This was not how his life was to be, he decided, but it was how God was laying it out for him. This lady needed his help. Only, that help didn't seem to be going anywhere.

"Roane? Where do we go from here? How do we track down whoever it is? I'm tired of not being able to live." Ragen blinked back tears. She was past the point where she could readily control her emotions.

`"I don't know. We're looking into everything that we can. For now? We may need to set it aside, but not forget it. There are men out there watching us. You received that letter. I have been getting emails and text messages on my business accounts that are threatening me, but not you. John and Jerome have those." Roane prayed even harder for his lady. He had finally acknowledged to himself that he loved this lady but had no idea how she felt. She was keeping that buried deeply. And Roane could understand that given how her life had been lived.

Ragen had turned to watch Roane as he spoke, seeing his feelings for her in his eyes. She wasn't sure what to think. This is not how she had expected to find someone. Ragen just couldn't comprehend that someone would be interested in her. That she was not marrying material had been drilled into her since her early childhood. And suddenly, Ragen realized that those words were wrong.

"We're heading for Mistletoe?"

"We are. I have friends there we can meet if you want. If not, then we just wander the town. I think there's a festival there this weekend. They have a special festival every month. I'll need to take you there for Christmas. It is a wonderful time to explore that town." Roane didn't hear his words, not understanding the hope and joy that was growing within Ragen as she listened to what his heart was saying to her.

Chapter 22

Walking through the town of Mistletoe, Ragen could feel her heart lightening somewhat. Her hand was tight in Roane's. She had looked at their hands and then at him. Roane had simply grinned and shrugged before he was tugging her along the sidewalk. Ragen was happy, for the moment, content to be with this man who seemed determined to protect her at all costs. She was just afraid of what those costs could mean.

Roane could feel the prickles in the back of his neck. They had been followed but he had not been able to determine which vehicle ist was. That scared him, he acknowledged. He wanted this to be a good day for his lady, without any danger, but that didn't seem to be happening.

Ragen's head was twisting and turning as she tried to take everything in. Her eyes studied the old buildings, liking what she was seeing.

"How old is this town, Roane?" She had to repeat her question before he answered her.

"I'm not sure. At least one hundred years." Roane paused at a store. "In here. Finn who owns this has lived her all her lives. She is a descendent of one of the founding families as is her husband, Jacob." The old-fashioned bell jingled as the door opened, bringing them to the attention of the young lady behind the counter. Her face lit up as she recognized Roane.

"Roane? You're in my town. Playing tourist or working?" Finn was around the counter to hug Roane and then surprised Ragen by hugging her too. "And who is this?"

"This is Ragen, a friend. Ragen, this is Finn. We've talked about her." Roane stepped back for a moment, watching closely as to how Ragen was reacting to Finn. He frowned even as he heard footsteps stop beside him and then turned his head to see Blackie, another friend from town, standing beside him. "Blackie?"

"Roane? You're in our town. Come for the festival or are you on the run?" Blackie grinned at him before he stepped forward to be introduced to Ragen.

Late that afternoon, Roane shut the car door after Ragen had seated herself. They had needed that break, he decided, a break away from everything just to forget for a few hours what was happening to them. He didn't see Simon, another friend, heading for his truck, intent on following them home. His wife, Eaven, was already waiting for him. Blackie and his wife, Julia, were ready to pull out in front of Roane. The four men from Mistletoe, all good friends, had decided among themselves that they would do this. Josh and his wife, Leah, and Finn, and her husband, Jacob, were meeting at Josh's home, just to pray the couple through a safe journey home. It was what they did.

Roane reached for Ragen's hand, his other hand steady on the steering wheel. He had been aware that someone had been following them all that day. His glance through the front window had him nodding. Friends were escorting them home. They didn't twice about doing that, he knew. Roane felt Ragen's fingers curling around his.

"Have fun today?" He grinned at the happy look on her face.

"I did. I have never done that before, you know, spent time like that with friends. I had no friends, only acquaintances. You have a wonderful set of friends." Ragen smiled but her heart hurt that she didn't have those friends and that once she was safe, she would just move on and lose contact with those friends.

"I do, and you are not leaving here. Do you know that?" Roane shook his head at the question on her face. "We'll talk, Ragen. For now, it is okay that you're hurting at what you didn't have. My friends welcome you into our group. We're spread far and wide and don't always see one another much. But I can guarantee that that group will work on what we are facing. Simon and Blackie work for Blackie's father, who is an investigator as well."

The two trucks parked at the curb and Blackie and Simon exited them, leaving the trucks running. Simon walked around the house and the garage, searching for anything that could have been left there that day with Roane being away. He didn't find anything but that didn't mean that no one had been around.

Blackie stood just inside the front door, listening to Roane walk through his house. Ragen had disappeared to her apartment, a quiet thank you to Blackie before she was gone from sight.

———

"Roane? Everything's okay?" Blackie watched his friend closely, seeing the subtle signs of stress and worry that were showing on his face.

"It seems to be. I'll check the video feed later. I can't thank you and Simon enough for taking time to guide us home." Roane stood for a moment, his hands jammed down into his jeans pockets.

"It's what we do, Roane. You would do the same for us. Listen. Dad is working on something that he came across that involves you. He hasn't said what as yet but he will be in touch or he'll send Simon or myself. We enjoyed today with you and Ragen." Blackie looked down, not sure how to phrase what he wanted to say.

"It's okay, Blackie. Ragen admitted that she had a good time today. It's sad, though, that she has had no friends. And I am just so afraid that she'll take off and we won't be able to find her." Roane was not hesitant to share his feelings.

"She'll try, but you won't let her. She has your heart, Roane, just as our ladies had ours." Blackie stepped to one side as the front door opened and Simon stepped inside. "All okay out there?"

"It is." Simon was puzzled. "I don't see that anyone has been around placing everything that they usually do. That tells me they are keeping a very close eye on you. Your office, Roane?" Simon waited patiently for Roane to look up and respond.

"I moved it here to the house. I just didn't feel safe there even though there was a lot of traffic around it. It would have been too easy for either Ragen or myself to disappear. She's working part time for me and part time in Dad's office." Roane looked up at the cream ceiling. "She's not talking a lot about what happened in her past. And she needs to."

"It will come. She's opening up to you, I think, Roane." Simon had no doubt that Ragen was beginning to feel freer and with that, she would open up to Roane. She was looking at him as her rescuer and that was exactly what he was.

"It will. I pray that it comes in time to prevent anything further from happening. But we all know that may not be the case." Roane turned his attention to his friends. "We need to meet once more with your father, Blackie. Emma is weighing in but hasn't found a lot right now. That's concerning."

"It is but she'll keep digging until she finds what she needs to. She always does." Simon shook Roane's hand and then disappeared, leaving Blackie staring at the floor.

"Blackie? You have a though?" Roane waited for Blackie to nod.

"I do. Are you sure that her parents are really her parents? Has anyone looked into that?" Blackie was hesitant to ask that but knew that would well be the case. Simon's wife, Eaven, had been abandoned as a newborn and adopted into a loving family. She was in fact sister to Blackie's wife, Julia, and cousin to Jacob's wife, Finn, and Josh's wife, Leah.

"I know your stories. Thanks for sharing them with Ragen. She needed to hear them." Roane drew in a deep breath. "Micah's Kat is tracing her family tree, Emma said.   She thought she might have information by early next week." Micah was one of the security team that Emma's husband, Abe, ran.

"She is? She's good at that. If she finds anything that we can help with, let us know.   You have many people working on this. Unfortunately, until we find that one piece of information that we need, we're in a holding pattern. I need to run. Call if you need us." Blackie was away at that, leaving Roane standing on his front porch, watching them drive away before his head dropped and he began to fervently beg God for a quick resolution to what Ragen was going through. He was afraid for his lady.

Chapter 23

Creeping towards the door of her apartment, Ragen carefully leaned forward to look through the window, keeping herself as hidden as she could. She had been certain that someone had been around the house earlier that day. Roane was away, testifying in court in another town for one of his cases. She was alone, this having been one of the days that she worked in his office. Ragen had done what she needed to and then sought solace in her apartment, her Bible in her hand as she searched for all the verses on joy that she could find. She drew in a deep breath of relief as she recognized Shaye.

"Shaye? You're here? Aren't you working today?" Ragen opened the door and pulled Shaye into the apartment,

"I took today off. God told me that you needed a friend today,". Shaye reached to hug her friend. ""Now, find your purse. You're coming with me. We're going to do some shopping and then find somewhere to have lunch." Shaye would not take no for an answer.

Ragen stared at her and then grinned. This was what she had been missing, she decided, spontaneous outings with friends. That had never been her lot in life. She breathed a quick prayer of thanks to God for providing her with friends.

Roane stared at his open front door mid-afternoon, suddenly afraid for his lady. He ran inside and searched, heading for the basement, and not finding Ragen. What he found was the broken in apartment door, His phone was out as he called for help, turning as he heard his name called. Rourke and Arin walked towards him, worry on their faces as they saw the door.

"Roane? What happened? Where's Ragen?" Rourke's arm rested across his son's shoulders as they stood on the sidewalk in front of the house. "Was she home?"

"She was to be. I didn't see her, Dad. Did they take her?" Roane blinked rapidly, his mind racing as to the possibilities of what had happened to his lady.

Arin paced away, her eyes on the traffic down the street. She frowned before she walked rapidly towards a vehicle that had stopped. Rowan walked towards his sister, reaching to hug her before he turned her to face her brother's house.

"What happened?" Rowan kept his voice low. He was worried about Roane and Ragen and that was why he had shown up.

"Ragen's missing. Roane said that the apartment door was broken in. He has no idea where she is." Arin struggled with her emotions. Ragen was becoming a sister to her and she was highly worried as well about her.

A voice spoke from behind them, startling them both. Rowan and Arin spun, to stare at the missing lady. Ragen stood there, Shaye and Slavin flanking her.

"Rowan? Arin? What happened? Why are you two standing here and not at the house? And why are there police here?" Ragen was puzzled. She had spent the day with Shaye before Slavin had joined them for a meal. She was on her way home, bags in her hands when she saw the activity around her home.

"Ragen? Where were you? Roane came home, found the house had been broken into, and couldn't find you." Rowan was shocked to see Ragen there.

"I was with Shaye and then with Shaye and Slavin. Shaye appeared this morning and rushed me away." Ragen's face paled. "If I had been home, would I have disappeared?"

Jerome had approached the group, recognizing Ragen as he did so.

"Ragen? What time did you two leave?" Jerome's voice beside her caused Ragen to jump in fear.

"Around 10, I think, wasn't it, Shaye?" Ragen turned to her friend, not seeing the dark look that had covered the men's faces.

"It was. God told me to find you and get you away from the house. This is why." Shaye began to shake for a moment, Slavin's arm around her. "If I hadn't obeyed God's nudge, you might not be here."

"God does that, sweetheart." Slavin's arm tightened around his wife. "And you have learned to obey."

Jerome nodded. It was not the first time that he had experienced that with a victim or witness. He prayed every day for safety for himself and his fellow detectives. Sometimes, one was hurt but so far, those injuries had been minor.

"Roane needs to know that you are safe." Jerome stepped away to speak into his radio, seeing John's hand raise in acknowledgement. "For now, we need to find somewhere for you to stay."

"I can't stay with anyone. I'm too dangerous." Ragen turned, ready to run, before she felt herself enveloped in strong arms that held her in place.

Roane had turned as John touched his arm, frowning at him.

"Roane? Ragen's safe. She's with your family, down the street." John waited for Roane to respond. When he didn't, John repeated himself.

Rourke turned his son away from his home and towards the street.

"Down there, son. She's with Rowan. Head that way." Rourke's gentle nudge had Roane shaking his head before he was running towards Ragen.

Roane's arms tightened even more as Ragen turned into his hug. He could feel the sobs shaking her body. His head rested on hers as he studied his friends and then his siblings who were there.

"Where were you?" Roane's question didn't bring an answer from Ragen. He turned instead to Shaye. "Shaye?"

"God sent me, Roane, to get Ragen away from here. If I hadn't gone when He told me to, she might not be here." Shaye was shaken as well by how God had led her to protect her friend.

"He does that." Roane turned slightly as he heard John's voice. "John?"

"We need to see your video feed, Roane. Can you come with us?" John gave a half smile as Roane turned towards his home, not letting go of his lady. Ragen kept step with him, not that she had much of a choice. Roane just was not letting go of his lady.

Chapter 24

John watched the video feed, Jerome standing beside him. He had asked Roane to leave the office, needing to watch it without him in the room. He paused the feed, staring at the men who were breaking into the apartment.

"They came prepared to break in." John pointed at the metal battering ram one of the men had in his hand.

"They did. And with a purpose. They are after Ragen. But we don't have a good idea as to why. Not yet, anyway. And until we do, we can't protect her the way we should." Jerome was frustrated at that. "We know those guys."

"We do. We've been after them for a while, haven't we? And it would be Roane and Ragen God is using to bring them to justice." John copied the feed that they needed onto a memory stick and then sealed it into an evidence bag. "From what the techs said, there is not a lot of evidence. The men were too careful."

"They were, but their faces are clear. Now to find them." John was on his feet, heading for his car, leaving Jerome to find Roane.

"Roane? We're done here for now." Jerome faced off against his friend. "You need to find somewhere to stay tonight. We're not releasing your house yet."

Roane sighed. It was what he had expected. Rourke had managed to convince Ragen to go with him to their home. She had been reluctant to do just that, wanting to stay with Roane but knowing that she needed to be safe.

"I'll head to Dad's. Ragen is there." Roane hesitated before he shook his head. "We can't take anything, can we?"

"Not right now." Jerome smiled in sympathy as Roane walked away, his head down in dejection and frustration. "Lord, be with my friends. Help us to solve this and soon. They need to find that joy in their lives once more."

Ragen turned from the shower, reaching for the clean clothes that Sofi had handed her. She needed to find that lady and thank her. Sofi was taking the place of the mother that she had never had. Ragen's hands stilled for a moment. She couldn't remember her mother caring much about her. That had always puzzled her but had also driven her deep into herself. That had made it hard for her to make friends.

Sofi turned as she heard soft footsteps, reaching to hug her son. Roane stood back from his mother, a hurt look on his face. Sofi could not change what had happened that day nor could she make it better for her son as she had when he had been a child. This was something that he had to work through with God's help. All she could do was pray for him.

"Roane? What now?" Sofi's voice brought Roane's attention back to his mother.

———

"I find someone to repair the door to the apartment and then find a cleaning team to go through. I talked with the insurance agent. He was around earlier when Jerome was still there. He's authorized me to go ahead with repairs once the house is released. Jerome said that an officer would be there overnight." Roane turned to wrap Ragen in his arms.

Ragen shoved away from Roane, not wanting to depend on anyone else but she was finding that hard to do. Roane was working his way into her life and heart. She just didn't know how she would ever walk away from him.

"Sofi? Thank you." Ragen's voice was soft and hesitant as she spoke. "I shouldn't be here. This is putting you and Rourke in danger."

"We don't look at it that way, Ragen. We are doing for you what we would do for our daughters. We think of you as our third daughter. I know. I know." She smiled at the younger lady. "Rowan and Ryley are dating but for now, you're our third daughter." Sofi caught the look on her son's face and nodded to herself. There was interest there, she decided. Now she knew how to pray for the couple and pray for them she would.

"Thank you, then." Ragen moved around the kitchen, finding a mug to fill with tea and then standing and staring down at the table. "What can I do to help?"

"What can you do? Just take care of yourself. Roane will help with that." Sofi felt free to speak her mind, Roane leaving to find his father. "He cares for you, Ragen. I don't know what your feelings are for him."

"I guess…" Ragen's voice died away for a moment. "I care for him, too, Sofi, and that scares me. I have never had any male friends. In fact, I didn't have any female friends. I was driven to hide inside myself." She looked up, blinking agains the tears. "And that was so wrong. Why did my parents treat me like that? I see your family and the joy that you have in one another. I never had that. I always felt that I was a burden. That's not how a child or teen should be raised. I guess that's why I left home at sixteen and then managed to get ahead on my own."

"No, it's not how you should be raised." Sofi sat beside Ragen, her hand gripping the younger lady's hand. "We can't change your past, but we can help you have a better future. That's how we are praying for you."

"Thank you." Ragen could barely speak for her emotions. "But how do we find out what's going on? Is it me or Roane? Or both of us? It just seems as if there are two parties involved."

"That's what Ryley is maintaining. I know he is working on that premise." Sofi raised her head as Artis and Arin appeared in the room, finding their own mugs of tea and then sitting down, just in solidarity with Ragen. "How be we have the soup that's ready? Then we can spend time in prayer. We need to cover you both with that." Sofi was on her feet, working to dish up the meal and then turning as her daughters had found the trays that were needed.

———

125

The men looked up from their papers as the ladies appeared, rising to take the trays. Their meal completed, the dishes were cleared away before they had gathered once more in the office, their heads bowing as they praying, seeking God's protection for the couple but also that they would find His joy in whatever circumstance they would themselves in.

Roane raised his head at last, his hand gripping Ragen's. She had made no move to pull it away from him and he frowned at that. He studied his family, seeing their determination in finding the culprits. He frowned at he noted that Slavin, Shaye, and Nickol had joined them as they had spent time before their Heavenly Father.

"What can we do?" Nickol spoke for the group. He held up papers that he had set to one side. "I have this. I don't know how it fits in but someone gave it to me and asked that I pass it on to Roane." He wouldn't give it to John or Jerome yet. He had been told not to. That when it was ready for the detectives, it would be given to them. Nickol was well aware that it was an undercover officer who had approached him.

Artis was on her feet, taking the papers and making copes for each one. There was silence in the room except for the rustling of the papers and the scratching of pens and pencils as notes were made. Rowan raised his head at last and then reached for his laptop. The woman named was prominent in town and seemed that she was honest. He had always had a bad feeling from her and now he could understand why. They would need to dig deep to find the proof but they would do that.

Ryley moved to sit on the floor beside his oldest brother, watching carefully as Rowan worked away.

"Her? It doesn't seem possible, does it?" Ryley sighed. "And we know that it's possible. How do we prove it?"

"I sent her name on to Emma. I haven't heard back but I think this is the week that they were away. She'll get back to us when she can." Rowan focused on Roane and Ragen. "It's going to be hard to keep those two safe, isn't it?"

"It will be. Ragen is finding freedom with Roane and she will not walk away from that." Ryley was on his feet, moving towards the kitchen, Arin with him. They needed a break from what they were working on and he knew that his mother would have cookies and squares that would help.

Chapter 25

A week later, Roane walked away from the courthouse in his town, his court filings done. He was free for the rest of the day and wanted to spend it with Ragen. Only, that lady was at work with his father. Roane had laughed as she had frowned at him that morning as he dropped her off at the office, telling him to go find something to do other than hovering over her. A smile had lurked in her eyes as she said that.

Turning as he heard his name called, Roane frowned at the two men walking towards him. Abe and Micah were there and that didn't mean good news, he decided.

"Abe? Micah? You're both here?" Roane pointed towards a nearby coffee shop, heading into it and then finding an isolated booth.

"We are." Abe's voice was light as he spoke but there was a sternness about his face that belied that lightness, "Emma sent us."

"I gathered that. How much?" Roane grinned as the two men laughed and Micah held up a thick envelope. "That much?"

"That much. She's worried about you two. And for Emma to be worried, that meant she sent us to find you. We just weren't expecting to find you walking down the street."

"No, I was just at the courthouse. Do we need to find Ragen?" Roane was ready to run from the shop to do just that.

"Not at present. We'll go over what we have, as much as we can here in public. Then, you can go over it with Ragen. You know what to look for in what Emma has provided. I can't promise, thought, that it will bring this to an end quickly."

Their conversation turned to what their families were up to before Abe simply prayed for his friend. Roane stood by his car, watching them walk away, the envelope clutched tight in his hands. He needed to find Ragen. A glance at his watch let him know that it was early to pick her up but that was exactly what he planned to do. Roane also wanted his father's input on what Emma had found.

Ragen turned as she felt arms around her, knowing that Roane had found her. She had been told to go home, a grin on Rourke's face as he said that. She had told him that she couldn't, that her ride was missing, and just as soon as she said that, Roane appeared.

"Roane? What happened?" Ragen could sense his uncertainty in how he held her.

"Abe and Micah were around. They brought information from both Emma and Kat that we need to go over." Roane looked over at his father, who still sat behind his desk, his hands folded on the desktop. "Dad? We'll need your input on it."

"Of course, son." Rourke glanced at his watch. "It's early, but Mom has supper ready. We'll eat, pray, and then look at it." He was on his feet, a hand resting on his son's shoulder before he disappeared from the room.

"Roane? What did they find? I can't wait that long." Ragen's voice held a touch of exasperation in it.

"We'll eat, Ragen. Then we'll spend time in prayer. We need that. I know that God is here around us, had His angels protecting us, but He will allow what is in His will for us to happen. We just need to trust him. I know how hard that is. We also need to find His joy in our circumstances. We are admonished to give thanks in all things. And that His joy is our strength." Roane's arms tightened around his lady. "We'll talk, Ragen. We'll talk. I don't want to lose you ever. I want you to stay in my life for the rest of our lives."

Ragen stilled as she heard his words, wonder on her face and happiness rising within her. She felt the same way about Roane but thought that it was too soon. She hadn't had parents who had modelled that type of love for her but she could see it with Rourke and Sofi, Slavin and Shaye, and with Roane's siblings with their significant others. Weddings were in the works for the other four but for now, she was content to be held by the man who was trying so hard to protect her.

"Roane? What did you just say? Did you mean that?" Ragen pushed away from him before she walked away, heading for the outdoors. Rowan followed her quietly, his eyes not on her but on the surrounding area, watching out for his brother's lady.

———

Roane stood in shock, thinking back on what he said. His hand hit the top of his head as his eyes slid closed. He did mean those words but he hadn't meant to say them as yet. He didn't think that Ragen was ready to hear them. Roane turned and walked from the house, to find the seat in the front yard where he had spent many hours as a youth, to think through what he was going through and try to determine just who it was who was after either him or his lady.

Sofi found her son not that long afterwards, sitting beside him on the bench in a motion that was reminiscent of how she had reacted to him as a youth.

"Need to talk, son?" Her arm went around him even as he was bent forward with his face buried in his hands.

"I don't know, Mom. I told Ragen that I didn't want her to leave ever. I don't know if this was the right time to say that or not." Roane straightened up, his eyes on his mother, seeing the understanding on her face.

"You do mean those words. And yes, it was not likely the best time to say that but Ragen needed to hear that. She is like a ship that is not anchored, moving with the tides. You are that anchor that she has been looking for, son. Whether you spend your lives together or not? That is up to God. He has walked this path before you and is leading both of you on it."

"I get that, Mom." Roane sighed. "It's just what we're going through. It's not making any sense no matter how we look at it. What if it isn't me? What if someone was after Dad or Rowan or Ryley? And with

Ragen? What if it's her parents driving this? We haven't been able to confirm much about them. Emma and Kat have tried but they're reaching dead ends. And that is not them." Roane was puzzled by that.

"That's what we were just discussing. You and Ragen needed to hear what that discussion was. Arin is adamant that Ragen's parents are using their correct names. She asked to see Ragen's birth certificate the other day and took a copy of it. She's not getting very far either. She has the same training as you and works closely with the women and children at the shelter. She should be able to find that information." Sofi grew pensive. "And it could be about someone other than you two. Or it could all be so intertwined that we can't find the right string to pull to determine just what it is."

"That's what I'm afraid of, Mom, that we won't find out in time and one of us is either seriously injured or killed." Roane was more sober than Sofi had ever seen him.

Chapter 26

Ragen turned as Rowan stopped beside her, his eyes dropping to study her face. She's stressed, he thought, and wondered just how they could solve this mystery.

"Rowan? Can I ask you something?" Ragen waited impatiently for Rowan to nod. "If this was you, what would you do? I can't go on much more like this. And it's not fair to Roane to be involved in danger because of me."

"Roane would be nowhere other than by your side. He cares deeply for you, in case you missed that." Rowan gave her a quick grin. "Now, what would I do? I would go back to my hometown and see what was happening there. We could do that for you, but you know your town. Or at least, you did."

"Why would you phrase it like that?" Ragen was puzzled at his words. She studied the yard around her, breathing deeply of the scents of the flowers around her.

"Because it's been what ten years or more since you were there? Towns change in that time. You would recognize the buildings and the people, but the undercurrents in town? Those would likely have changed." Rowan had been in contact with another friend of the family who had travelled to her town and walked through it, talking to those he needed to speak with. That report from his friend was due to be sent the next day. "I had a friend walk through your town.

He is sending me a report tomorrow. And yes, you and Roane will receive copies. We see what he has to say and then plan from there." Rowan turned her back towards the house. "For now? We need to get you out of sight. Someone is out there, just waiting for you to be out here on your own. If you are, you disappear. Roane doesn't deserve to have his lady in danger of disappearing." Rowan gently nudged her back to the house and then inside before he was walking the yard, nodding as he saw evidence that someone had been waiting there near the back of the yard and had escaped through their neighbour's yard. He would contact that family the next day and ask to see their video feed. There may be something on it, he thought, that would identify who had been there.

Late that night, Roane sighed to himself. He was unable to sleep and had been working through some of his investigations. He dropped the pen he was holding to his desktop before he buried his head into his hands, drawing a deep breath as he did so. Something just didn't seem right with what they were going through, him and Ragen. And he was so afraid for his lady. On his feet, Roane reached for his filing cabinet from his office, searching through the folders before his hand stopped at one particular folder. He withdrew it and then returned to his desk to drop into his chair, the closed folder on the desk. Roane was afraid suddenly, more afraid than he had ever been. When he opened that folder, he was sure that he would have more understanding on what had happened to Ragen.

Hearing a sound at his back door, Roane walked carefully that way, careful to not put on any lights. He stared at the dark form standing there before a light shone on the man's face. Roane reached to unlock the door, opening to draw the man inside.

"Bill Buckley? What are you doing here?" Roane stared at his detective friend from Elmton.

"Looking for you. Andrew asked me to find you." Bill held up a folder. "We came across some information early this evening that we had to verify before I headed here." He sighed, deeply troubled by what they had confirmed but also exhausted. It had been a long day, a day that he had hoped to spend the evening with his wife and son and daughter. That hadn't happened.

"I see." Roane turned to the kitchen counter. "Let me put on a fresh pot of coffee. And then find something for us to eat. I would assume that you haven't had a meal yet."

Bill nodded, grateful for the offer of food.

"That would be wonderful, Roane. Thank you." Bill eyed his friend. "How are you holding up?"

Roane shrugged before he turned to face Bill.

"About how you were. How do we find the ones involved?" Roane knew that Bill, like many of their friends, had undergone an adventure with his wife, Cora, that had almost killed them. Bill's first wife had been killed by a new designer drug, Cora's first husband the one who had dealt that deadly blow. He had in turn be killed just as he and Cora had married.

"We work through what we have. It's going to be a long night." Bill turned as he heard soft footsteps as Ragen approached.

———

"Ragen?" Roane walked towards her, a frown on his face. She usually didn't use the door that opened into the front hall of his home.

"Roane? We need to solve this. I'm so afraid." Ragen was terrified. She was sure that she had heard someone calling out to her, that she would be dead by morning. "I thought I heard someone outside my bedroom window, telling me I would die."

Bill set his mug down and reached for the back door, his hand on his weapon, taking with thanks the large flashlight being handed to him. He walked slowly around this house, the flashlight glancing off the house walls before he stopped near a basement window. Bill nodded to himself. Someone had been there. Ragen had not imagined what she had heard. He pulled out his phone, staring at it for a moment. This was not his town but he knew Jerome from past task forces. He stepped away from the house, walking the yard as he spoke with that town's emergency dispatch.

Roane seated Ragen before he crouched down beside her, an arm around her. He looked up as the door opened and then closed. Bill gave a brief nod, causing Roane to sigh.

"Ragen, is it?" Bill's voice startled Ragen who stared at him, fear on her face. "I'm a friend from another police force. The name's Bill Buckley. And you were not imagining anything. There was someone outside of your bedroom window. I have called it in for you, Roane." Bill leaned back against the counter, hearing the tap at the back door before it opened to allow Jerome to enter.

———

"Bill? You're here?" Jerome was somehow not surprised at that.

"I am. I have information for you as well but I wanted to speak with Roane and Ragen too." Bill sighed to himself once more before he began to pray for his friends. This was when it became dangerous for them, he knew, and there wasn't anything that they could to do prevent that danger from approaching them. Only God would and could be their Shield. Bill also know how hard it was to find joy in what they were facing.

Chapter 27

Jerome stepped back inside the house, squinting at his watch as he did so. It was early morning already and he had been on his feet since early morning the day before. He had not expected to be called out as he had and find Bill there. Jerome's head tilted for a moment as he listened and then nodded. Ragen was asking the questions of Bill that she needed to. She had not asked them but given that he was friends with Roane and his family, that could explain it. Bill was a stranger to her and had the ability he had seen in few to be able to draw out information from crime victims.

"Ragen? Why would you ask what you just did? You asked if you were the child of your parents." Bill had heard something like this many times. It was not uncommon for victims to ask that.

"I don't know." Ragen rubbed at her eyes. She was exhausted and not really thinking all that clearly. She leaned back against Roane, who had his arm around her as they sat on the couch in his office. Ragen really didn't want to look at the material that Bill had brought to them. She had had no choice but to go over. She was surprised at the information on her family, information that she had never known. "What did you mean when you said that Mom was estranged from their families? I can remember even up to when I left home that their parents were around."

"Those were not their parents. I've been in your home town, Ragen. Rowan asked that of me. This is the report that he was expecting me to send to him.

Instead, my police chief, Andrew, asked that I come in person." Bill watched Ragen as her face crumpled, a sympathetic look on his face.

"They weren't? I don't understand. Who were they?" Ragen's hand clutched at Roane's, finding his arms tight around her, trying his best to comfort her.

"That is what your town's police are now working on. They will work with Jerome and John here in this town." Bill watched Ragen closely, seeing the puzzlement and bewilderment that she was feeling. "Talk to me, Ragen. Tell me what you can."

Ragen shook her head. Whatever she had expected to hear in the report, this had not been it. And she had not expected other police forces to become involved.

"Why? Why would they do that?" Ragen bit at her lip, growing angry that her life had been like it was. "Is that why someone wanted to find me? To take me back and make me live a lie again?"

Roane was nodding. He had read through Bill's report as quickly as he could, picking up the main points as he did so.

"It would seem so. It looks as if they contacted me to find you and bring you to them so that they could do just that. I was used." Roane had to tamp down his own anger at that, knowing that he would be working that anger through with his Heavenly Father. "Bill? What else?"

"What else? Ragen is missed. Her mother never said. In fact, she has refused to speak about you,

Ragen. It's as if you never existed in her life. I do know that the police in your town served a search warrant on her home. There is no evidence that you ever lived there."

Ragen stared at Bill in shock, who gave her a small smile. Her head turned to Jerome who was watching her as well, sympathy on his face. She looked past him to see Rourke and Sofi had appeared, called in by Jerome who knew that Ragen needed them. Sofi simply sat beside Ragen and wrapped her in mother's arms, a hug that Ragen leaned into. Ragen decided that she had never had a hug like that. In fact, she had never been hugged by a mother. She had been tolerated.

"Why? Who was behind this?" Ragen's words stopped any movement in the room. She had asked the question that the authorities were asking with no answer apparent at the time.

"We are working on that, Ragen. It takes time to find that out." Jerome sighed to himself, stifling a yawn. He was exhausted but couldn't show it. Ragen needed his investigative talents and experience at this time and he would do no less for her than he would for any other victim.

"Thank you. What can I do to help?" Ragen would not sit back and wallow in her sorrow and pain any more. She was determined to solve the mystery of her life and do it that day if at all possible.

"We need a list of anyone and everyone that you can think of who had contact with this couple. A list of your friends and acquaintances. A list of any business owners or professionals that you may suspect of being involved." Bill grinned at the look of shock on her face that turned to a look of determination.

Ragen reached for the pad of paper and pen that Roane was handing her. Her attention was on the names that she was listing, not hearing the conversation and movement in the room around her.

Bill rose at last, heading for the door. He needed to be on the road, having to be in court that morning.

"Call me, Jerome. I want to solve this for them." Bill stood for a moment, his head tilted back as he prayed for Roane and Ragen. This was when it always became so dangerous, he thought.

"I will. I'll get the list to you or Andrew." Jerome needed to head off too, his shift ending, but he didn't want to. Common sense prevailed and he too walked for his vehicle, reaching to read the text messages that had arrived. He nodded once more. John had arrived at the office, finding a lot of documentation that Emma had sent on for them.

John stared down at his desktop and the folders there. He couldn't devote all of his time to this case, he had more than this one on his desk, despite his desire to work it through. He reached for the top folder, his pen out as he made notes and then reaching for the next one. His supervisor stood for a moment, watching John working away before he nodded to himself. John was proving that he was a dedicated police officer, determined to solve each and every case that he was involved in.

———

Chapter 28

Ragen paced Rourke's office. They had all gathered there, working through the report that Bill had provided and then through the information that Emma had sent on. She was puzzled and worried and that showed in the abrupt movements that she was making. Artis and Arin shared a look before they linked arms with Ragen and pulled her from the room to the kitchenette and sat her down at the table. They simply bowed their heads and prayed for Ragen, Arin begging God to solve this mystery and let Ragen live in joy the life that she should.

Artis looked around as she heard a noise at the back door and was on her feet, opening it. A small scream was stifled as she saw the armed men standing there, pointing at the three ladies. The ladies rose, knowing that they could well be shot if they refused the men's silent commands, heading out of the door and then for the delivery van that was waiting.

Ragen reached for the other ladies' hands as they were shoved to a sitting position on the floor, their hands tight on each other's. Blindfolds were tied tightly around their faces, not allowing them to see the direction that they were travelling. The men had taken care that their faces had been covered, preventing the women from seeing much. Ragen frowned even as she feared for their lives. The men had not worn gloves and that seemed to be a mistake. She tucked away the evidence on the hands and lower arms of the men, knowing that she needed to do that and be ready to give those details to Jerome or John. Ragen had no doubt that they would be able at some point to identify the men.

Ryley was on his feet, searching for the ladies and not finding them. He frowned and then hit the front door, searching for them. Returning to the office, he was almost running for the computer that held their security system, hearing footsteps behind him.

"Ryley?" Rowan rested a hand on his brother's shoulder. "What are you up to? And where are the ladies?"

"They're not here. Artis' car is still in the parking lot." Ryley grew silent as fear grew within him as he found the section of the video feed that he needed. He felt Rowan's hand tighten on his shoulder. "There. Someone has them."

"I see." Rowan made the call that they had prayed that they would never have to make. "John? The ladies have disappeared. Gunmen took them from the kitchen area." Rowan turned as he heard his father's footsteps and shook his head at him.

Rourke stopped his forward walk, fear growing within him. He listened to Rowan's conversation with John as he stood, his own hand on Ryley's shoulder. He pointed suddenly.

"Ryley? What's that?" Rourke's attention was on the van. "It's a delivery van. What's that decal?"

Ryley was nodding, reaching to print off a still photo of the van and then enlarging it.

"It's a horse, Dad. Who do we know who has that delivery company?" Ryley looked up at his father, seeing the nod that Rourke was giving.

"We know that company, Ryley. In fact, we turned down work recently for them." Rourke almost ran for the filing room, pulling open a filing cabinet drawer and retrieving a file. He turned back to find Roane standing in front of him.

"Dad? What's going on? Rowan said that Ragen, Artis, and Arin are missing." Ragen was becoming more and more worried.

"They are. We have a picture of the men and van that they disappeared into." Rourke handed over the file. "This company." He looked around Roane at that point and frowned at Ryley. "Ryley?

"Dad? The men were careless. We have enlarged pictures of tattoos on their hands and forearms. I have printed off copies for us and for John." Ryley could hardly stand still, he just wanted to be out there and searching for his sisters and Roane's lady.

"You do? Is John here yet?" Rourke laid an arm across the shoulders of his two sons who stood beside him, watching Rowan as he hesitated in the doorway.

"He is. He has a crime scene team in the kitchenette. We need to leave." Rowan turned away, heading for the front door, reaching to hug his mother who had appeared, sensing that something was wrong with her family.

———

John stared down at the photos, before he turned to Jerome.

"Jerome? We know these men. We've been looking for them for other crimes." John tilted the photo towards the other detective.

Jerome reached for it, studying it in turn.

"We do. Only we have no idea where they are." He looked around. "Rourke has a name for the company, Rowan said. Someone is working on their statements?"

"They are." John was frustrated at the turn of events. "We need to find the ladies. Artis and Arin were likely taken just because they were there." He frowned as Jerome shook his head. "You don't think so."

"No. For some reason, this comes back to Rourke and his paralegal work. Artis and Arin would have been taken to bring pressure on him for some reason. And Ragen would have disappeared because of what she is facing and what Roane is involved in. Somehow, this all is connected with the family and with Ragen's family or non-family, however you want to look at it." Jerome watched as the crime scene techs worked away. "We need to solve this soon and bring the ladies home. I fear for them."

"Me too. I know that God is in control but sometimes the darkness seems to be winning." John was discouraged, an emotion that hit all the detectives at some point in any investigation.

"He is.   We need to remember that He has walked this path before us all and that He only allows what is in His will for us."   Jerome walked away, needing to be at another crime scene.   He had been called in from his off time, one of the other detectives facing emergency surgery for a sudden illness.

John watched him walk away, acknowledging that his words were true before he turned as a tech approached him.

"Rob? What do you have?" :John reached for the evidence bag. "What's this?"

"An earring. I don't know if it belongs to one of the ladies or not. Do they have pierced ears?" Rob looked around, knowing that they had found all the evidence that they could but still wanting to find more.

"No, none of them do. Artis said one time that neither she or Arin could stand the thought of sticking something into their earlobes. I haven't seen Ragen wearing any. In fact, she doesn't have the marks on her ears from piercings." John nodded. "Someone else has been around here. This is not a cheap earring. It looks as if it's a real diamond."

"That's what we think. We'll test if for DNA and then store it in evidence. Find the lady who lost it and we'll match it."   Rob walked away, leaving John standing with a contemplative look on his face.

Chapter 29

Ragen paced the office that the three ladies were locked in. She had tried the door multiple times as had Artis and Arin, finding it locked up tight. She had reached for the windows, not able to raise them. She frowned. They were on the main floor of a building. Ragen just didn't know where it was.

"Where are we? Do either one of you know?" Ragen huddled close to the sisters, keeping her voice as low as she could.

"We do, unfortunately. This is the deputy mayor's office. He has a business that involves courier work. Why would he be involved?" Artis walked the edge of the room, trying to find any information that she could to help them understand why they were where they were. A letter on the desk caught her eye and she frowned as she read it, reaching for her phone to take a photo of it. Artis stared at her phone, frowning even harder. She spun to walk rapidly back to the other two. "They didn't take our phones."

"No, they didn't. They are waiting for us to use them and then they'll move us." Arin reached for her sister's phone, to tuck it into that lady's pocket. "Keep it away. I don't know what you found but we need to be very careful."

Ragen shrugged, not sure what Arin was meaning but knowing that she was likely correct in her suppositions.

———

"Talk to me, ladies. Tell me about this man." Ragen found a seat, pointing to nearby chairs. "Who is he? And why take us? I don't understand that."

"There have been rumours for years about him. Dad, I think, has had run-ins with him in the past. He has kept us as far away from him as he could. As to his business? He runs a courier company, which has been rumoured to be used to transport stolen items. No one has ever been able to prove that." Artis turned to Arin as Arin snorted at her last words.

"The streets are filled with those rumours. I know that the authorities have been trying for years to link him to the thefts and disappearance of luxury items. No one has done that." Arin sighed. "And it falls on us to do just that."

Artis gave a grim smile before she was on her feet, finding pads of paper and pens that she had no reluctance to take and use. She was handing them back to the ladies.

"Here. Write out what we know. Then, we hide them in our shoes." Artis scratched away at her own pad of paper, finally tearing off the papers and stuffing them into her shoes, finding her sister and Ragen doing the same. She was on her feet to return the pads of paper and pens to where she had found then, hoping against all odds that no one had a camera in the room and had seen what they had just done.

The sudden clicking of the lock had the ladies jumping and then turning to face the door. It barely cracked open, only enough for a hand to reach through and drop a bag of food on the floor. Water bottles followed, leaving the ladies staring at the bags, the bottles and then the locked door.

"Did someone really do that?" Ragen carefully approached the bags and reached for the water bottles. "Can we trust that the food or water is not tampered with?"

"We don't know that. God knows and He will not let any harm come to us." Arin reached for a bottle and felt around it. "I don't think it has been tampered with." She opened it and sipped watching as Artis and Ragen did the same. "The food? What is it?"

Artis reached for the bags, opening it to find vending machine sandwiches.

"I doubt these are tampered with but I don't trust that. I'm not really that hungry." She set the bag of food to one side. "Let's leave it for now. We need to find our prayer corner, ladies, and spend our time here before our Father. He is the One who will free us."

Hours passed. Day turned to night and then to day and then to night again. The only contact that the ladies had with anyone was when the door would crack open just enough for food and water to be dropped on the floor. The ladies would exchange a glance when this happened, Ragen studying hard what she could of the hand and wrist, memorizing the tattoos that were there. Their constant prayer was for release and then for the family. The sisters were worried about their siblings and parents and then the extended family. They were fully aware that everyone would be out there looking for them, putting them into danger to do just that.

———

Ragen was worried as well but her mind had cleared from that enough for her to think through her early life and the people in it. She was sure that somehow her parents were involved in this, whatever this was that she was involved in and that now involved her friends. She needed to find her freedom to prove it.

Three more days passed, long empty days. The three ladies talked among themselves, no closer to finding out who it was that had kidnapped them. No one had appeared to ask anything of them and that puzzled the three. They were sure that someone should have been there, asking something of them or demanding that they become involved in something. That had not happened.

"We need to get out of here." Ragen paced the room that afternoon, her hands clenched into fists. There was no option in her mind. They had to get away. Just how that would happen, she didn't know, but she could feel the growing fear in her heart that if they didn't, one of them or all three of them would either disappear or die.

"I know." Artis was pacing the room as well, turning as she heard a soft sound, a frown on her face as she spun in a circle before she watched Arin approaching a window. She frowned even harder at the man who appeared there. Artis knew him as a street person, not realizing that he was in fact an undercover officer.

"Arin?" Artis' hand clutched at her sister's arm, feeling Ragen's hand clutching at hers. "How do we get out of here?"

The officer held a finger to his lips before he disappeared. A soft sound came at the door as the lock clicked open and the officer appeared, beckoning the ladies forward. They rushed towards him and through the door, not seeing that he closed and locked the door behind them before he was ahead of them and leading them from the house and towards safety. A group of his friends moved in to surround the ladies, hustling them as rapidly as they could towards the centre of town and to a building that looked dilapidated but was in fact a secure place to hide the ladies until they could be gotten to their loved ones.

The three ladies stared at one another, shock on their faces before they turned to the officer, a man named Michael.

""”You’re safe, ladies. We’ll get you home as soon as we can. For now, though, we need to keep you here and out of sight.” Michael walked away, knowing that his friends would stand guard. He turned his phone over in his hands before he dialled a number. “John?”

“Michael? Why are you calling me?” John stood at the edge of yet another crime scene, his attention not totally on the call.

“I have the three ladies, John. I’ll get them to you as soon as I can and it’s safe.” Michael tucked his phone away, not hearing John asking for more information.

John stared at his phone before he looked up at Edward, a patrol officer who had been investigating the scene with him. Edward gave him a puzzled look, listening as John simply stated that the three ladies were free.

Chapter 30

Turning as he heard a soft sound, Roane barely had time to brace himself before a body hit him, arms wrapping tight around him as the lady began to sob, huge, heart-broken, fear-filled sobs. His own arms wrapped around Ragen, his heart breaking for his lady. He had no idea where she had just come from but he glad that she was there. Roane stared at his sisters as his father held them, their own sobs sounding loud in the sudden silence of the room. Michael had tracked the family down at Rourke's home, shoving the ladies inside and then disappearing to somewhere he could monitor the home.

John stood beside Michael where he had hidden himself, his own eyes watchful.

"Where were they?" John's voice was barely audible.

"Where we suspected. At Olde's home on the outskirts of the downtown area. He had them locked into an office in that home. Someone came forward this morning with word as to where they were. I went and found them. They'll need help, John." Michael nodded towards the house before he was running from where he had been hidden and tackling a man to the ground.

John flew after him, helping to haul the man to his feet.

"Jason Olde. What are you doing here? This is not your home area." John's voice was stern. As far as he knew, Jason was not rumoured to be involved in any crimes.

"I just found out about the ladies. Dad has been away for the last few days. I happened to hear one of his men saying something about the other house and the locked room. I wanted to go in and find them but I couldn't go there. Dad would have me killed if I did." Jason Olde was almost in tears. He was just eighteen and still young in street smarts.

"It's okay, Jason. We know that you're not involved." John nodded as Michael slipped away. "Come with me. We'll put you somewhere you'll be safe. What about your mom and sister?"

"They're away, out of town. Mom has moved away and taken Jayne with her." Jason rubbed at his eyes. "I was supposed to go too but I didn't. Something kept me here." He slumped in John's patrol car seat, devastated at what his father had done. "Where am I to go?"

""For now, I'll take you to the department. One of the detectives will talk with you. And then, we'll find somewhere we can hide you away. We'll do our best to keep you safe, Jason. That's a promise." John made that promise, not knowing if he could really do that. "You need to tell us all that you know about your father and his activities."

Jason nodded, before he held up his phone. He stared at it, blinking back his tears.

"I have documents stored on a cloud program that Dad doesn't know about. Mom pays for my phone. Dad wanted access to it but we didn't let him.

That was just last week. I've been hiding away from home since then. Mom and Jayne left at that point and I have only had text messages from them. We're afraid that Dad would find them. I have not had a nice life." Jason didn't look at John, not wanting to see pity on the older man's face.

John gave a grim smile, his eyes full of compassion for the teen. He should not have lived a life like it seemed he had. His youth had been stolen from him and he would never get it back.

Jerome stood and watched as John ushered Jason into an interrogation room, left and then returned with a bottle of water for the youth before he spoke with one of the lady detectives. That lady nodded and entered the room, the door closing quietly behind her. John turned to find Jerome, not having heard him approach him.

"John? I know that you have officers at Rourke's. What happened?" Jerome pointed towards the break room, needing a cup of coffee to make up for the lunch and supper that he had missed.

"The ladies are home. Michael came through." John stirred his coffee. "I need to head back there. While I was talking with Michael, we found Jason Olde watching the house. He has information on his father that he wants to give us. Then, we need to find some place to hide him."

"We'll come up with something. Abe Finlay has been in touch. He has Jason's mom and sister there and will come through with some of his team to move Jason that way." Jerome rubbed at the back of his neck. "You have no idea what happened to the ladies?"

"Other than what little Michael has said. He found them locked into an office in one of Olde's building near the downtown." John moved away, heading for his car to head back towards Rourke's home. His face grew grim as he watched the vehicle following him before a patrol car moved in and stopped it.

Rourke stood on his front porch, watching as John climbed the steps and then stopped beside the man who had become a good friend of his over the years. John prayed for his friend and his family, knowing that with the ladies escaping, their lives were likely in danger. From what little they could tell them, they were no able to state why they had been taken. Nothing had been asked from them, which puzzled everyone.

"Rourke? What can we do for you and your family?" John looked past him at the front door of the house before he turned to watch the street, the evening sounds of nature ringing in his ears.

"What can you do?" Rourke shrugged, an arm coming around Sofi who had come to find him. "I don't know, John, to tell you the truth and to be honest. We'll find someone for the girls to speak with. Someone has already reached out to us, a friend of Emma's. But what can you tell us?"

"Not a lot, not at the moment. We're investigating the man responsible and have the address where they were held. It will take time, Rourke. All we can do for now is try to keep you and the ladies and the rest of your family safe." John looked around at the number of cars parked around the area. "Your parents and siblings are here?"

"They are. They will not stay away, not even if they're in danger, they will not stay away. You know that only too well." Rourke gave a quick smile as he pondered the love of his family. "God is here, John. He will guide us and help us to find His joy that He provides in all circumstances."

John nodded before he moved past the older couple, heading inside the house. He could hear the conversation coming from different rooms and stopped beside the three brothers, who were watching their sisters and Ragen intently.

Chapter 31

Wrapping a blanket around herself hours later, Ragen curled up on the sofa at Rourke's home. She didn't feel safe, not even there and knowing that there were police officers outside for the night. She didn't know if she would ever feel safe and happy again. Any joy that she had had in life seemed to have disappeared and she had no idea how to find it again.

Roane slept in a nearby chair, his lack of sleep from the last few days more than he could cope with. His sleep was broken, his movements restless as he twisted and turned in the chair, unable to drop into a deep sleep. Rowan watched first Ragen and then Roane, knowing that whatever it was they were involved in was not over and that it had just become that much more dangerous for them.

Ragen finally rose, the blanket still wrapped around herself and walked quietly to the office, reaching for some of the material that had been amassed over the last few days. Rowan followed her, waiting patiently for Ragen to ask her questions that he just knew that she would. He just didn't know if he had the answers that she would require and demand.

"Rowan? What do we know about my family? Am I really theirs?" Ragen looked up at him, a lost look on her face but determination as well to find out the answers.

"No, we don't think that you are. Emma had a lead that she was following up regarding that but her comments were that you're not. We won't know for sure until she finds the information to confirm that either way. As to your family, we are finding out more information on them. Bill had been sending what he has verified and that he can release to us. As you know, some information has to stay within the investigation until it goes to trial."

Ragen nodded, her hands clasped on her knee. Her gaze was intent on Rowan as he spoke.

"What else? I have accepted the fact that they are not my parents or if they are, that I was never wanted. Do you know how much that hurts?" Ragen didn't cry. Her tears had dried up for now.

"I don't know that, Ragen. I'm sorry that you weren't raised in a family that loved you. Roane was. We have our squabbles but nothing serious enough to break our family ties. We support one another. We can tell that Roane has chosen you for his lady, Ragen." Rowan's hand went up as her mouth opened. "It is true. He'll talk with you at some point but we can see how he feels. For now? Set that aside and pray it through. Now, we need to work through that pile of papers you're holding. Dad has moved in some white boards for us and we have put the highlights and confirmed information on it." Rowan nodded towards those very boards. "Read through it and we'll talk." Rowan was on his feet, heading to find Ragen something to eat, even if it was just toast and something to drink. He nodded as he pulled out the orange juice. This was exactly what she needed, he decided.

Ragen took with thanks the food that Rowan handed her. A puzzled look covered her face.

"How is Roane really doing?" Ragen was afraid to hear what Rowan would say.

"He's hurting, Ragen, simply because you disappeared on our watch and he could not prevent it. He's hurting because you and Artis and Arin disappeared for a few days, days that we can never get back with you three. He's hurting because he can't solve this. Roane is hurting for you because of the life you have been forced to live, particularly in the last few years. He wants to make it all better for you but understands that he can't." Rowan was kept under Ragen's steady gaze as she listened to him. "He's hurting because he wants to find and choose joy in a life with you and for now that's not possible. He wants you to make your own choice and that doesn't seem possible at the moment."

Ragen nodded, knowing that was how she also felt to some extent. She had regressed somewhat into herself when she was held captive but had prayed that through. Ragen was determined to choose joy in her life and if Roane was part of that, she could and would accept that was God's will for her life.

"I don't want to run away any more, Rowan. I want to solve this and then find the life that God has for me. I want to choose His joy in my life. I don't have to like what I go through or what my friends go through but I know that God will protect us." Ragen was on her feet, heading for the white boards. "Talk to me, Rowan. Tell me what is here and what I need to know and what I can tell you."

Rowan nodded. Ragen was reacting as they had prayed that she would. His head turned slightly as he heard footsteps heading their way, stumbling slightly before Roane appeared, heading to wrap his lady into his arms.

Ragen stiffened for a moment before she shoved away from him. She couldn't do this right now, she decided, and then walked away, leaving Roane staring after her, a hurt look in his eyes before he shuttered them.

Rowan watched his brother closely before he sighed. This was what they had expected but prayed wouldn't happen. Ragen was hiding, he decided, and that needed to stop.

"Roane? What can we do for you?" Rowan waited patiently for his brother to bring his attention to him.

"What can you do for me?" Roane shrugged. "I have no idea, Rowan. I truly don't. I want this over. Ragen needs to know who has been after her and why."

"And so do you. Somehow, you two have been connected by someone and I want to know who and why." Rowan paced the small area around his brother. "How do we do that, Roane?"

Roane shrugged before he moved away, heading for the back deck and fresh air. He felt stifled for some reason, as if he was in a vacuum that was sucking all the air from his lungs. His head tilted back and his eyes closed as he began to pray for his lady. He had no idea if she would ever accept him as her boyfriend and maybe groom. All he could do was beg God for a chance to approach her.

Ragen watched from the safety of her kitchen door, knowing that she needed to approach Roane but reluctant to. She had no words to say, to ask what she needed to. Her hand shook as she stared at her phone before she turned and walked away from the door behind her. Ragen felt as if she needed to make plans to disappear. Only if she did that Roane would follow her and that frightened her, given what they had already faced.

Chapter 32

Running through the heavy rain, Roane fingered the key fob, clicking it to unlock the door of his truck. Safely inside, he hesitated before he reached to lock the door. This was unusual for him. Roane usually waited for the doors to look as the truck picked up speed. Today? He felt that he had to lock himself inside of it. Someone was out there and watching him closely, almost too close to him. He could almost feel the hand on his coat as he had run for his truck.

Dropping the bag that he held to the floor on the passenger's side, Roane hesitated. He squinted through the windshield and sighed. It was raining too hard to drive away, that much he knew. His phone was out as he sent a message to his client, asking to meet on the next day. Roane frowned as he didn't get a response. That was unusual for that client. The chiming of his phone startled Roane for a moment before he was reading the message. His client had responded at last.

Finally the rain relented enough so that Roane could drive away. He gave a grim smile as a truck pulled out behind him, almost too close to his own truck. He turned abruptly down a narrow street, knowing just where he was heading. The truck following him didn't have time to respond.

Arriving at his father's business, Roane was running for the door, closing it behind him, the bag of food in his hand handed over to Rowan.

"Roane? What just happened?" Rowan stared at his brother before he was at the door, cracking it open to study the parking lot.

"Someone was following me. I managed to ditch them but they'll be back." Roane paced. "Have you heard from Ragen today?"

"No, we haven't. Haven't you?" Rowan was surprised at Roane's question.

"No, I haven't. And that worried me." Roane was out of the building and running for his truck, Rowan keeping pace with him. "Where would she be?"

"At home and ignoring you?" Rowan gave a quick smile at the glare Roane directed towards him. Sobering, he began to pray for his brother and his lady, begging God for protection for them both.

*If she isn't, I need to find her." Roane squinted through the windshield, the wipers working at full speed to keep the glass clear. "I don't like this, Rowan."

"We know that you don't. We're working on it, bro, just haven't got it all figured out yet." Rowan was deeply worried about his brother, unable to fully express his feelings.

"I know that." Roane drew in a deep breath. "We're not sure which one of us it is."

"We don't." Rowan hesitated to speak. "Artis and Arin are trying to convince us that it's you, that you were chosen to find Ragen for some reason that would reflect back on you. Only, you have been too careful in how you've treated her." He twisted in his seat to stare at his brother. "Who would want to do that, to discredit you? Which of your recent cases or even any case would have that person contacting you again?"

Roane drew in a deep breath. Rowan's words had just congealed his own thoughts.

"I thought of that, Rowan, and have been working on that. We need to stop at my home but first I need to find Ragen." Roane was twisting the key from the ignition and running for the back yard, intent on knocking at Ragen's door. He just wasn't expecting to find her standing, framed in the doorway, waiting for him. "Ragen?"

"Roane? You're okay?" Ragen threw herself into his arms, sobs shaking her body. Rowan reached for the piece of paper crumpled in her right hand, gently loosening her fingers to retrieve it.

"Ragen?" Roane was desperate to find out what had disturbed his lady but she just wouldn't let go of him. A hand on his back moved the couple into the apartment and the door closed behind them.

Rowan stared at the paper he held, a sharply indrawn breath his only reaction. It was brutal, he decided, not what he had ever expected to be directed towards his brother despite his brother's occupation. His phone was out as he called John, having to leave a voice mail only. That was not what he wanted but he shrugged, It was what it was. Rowan looked up at his brother, his heart breaking for him. All he could do at present was pray, begging God to protect Roane and Ragen.

"Ragen?" Roane was finally able to reach through her terror with his voice.

Ragen stepped back, her arms wrapping around herself, clutching the blanket closer that she had wrapped around herself.

"Roane? Make them stop. Please! I can't do this." Ragen moved back away from him as he reached for her again, his arms dropping to his side.

"Rowan? What did that paper say?" Roane had caught a quick glimpse of something in Ragen's hand as he had wrapped her close to him.

"Threats, Roane. Threats against you. Remember what I asked? How close was I to the truth?" Rowan moved away to answer the door, letting in John, who removed his jacket and cap to hang them on the hooks near the door.

"Ragen?" John slowly approached the lady. "When did you get that?"

"Maybe thirty minutes. I don't know for sure." Ragen squinted at the clock. "Not much more than that. I tried to find Roane but he wasn't home even though he did come to my door just now." Ragen frowned at Roane. "How did you know?"

Roane shrugged. He couldn't explain how he knew. God had sent him towards her, that much he knew.

"I just sensed that you were in danger. God sent me towards you. Rowan was with me." Roane frowned at her. "What was in that letter?" He reached to take it from John, ignoring that man's frown. He read it, his face paling for a moment before determination filled his heart to bring this to a close. "John? How do we find whoever this is? And bring this to a stop? I have a lady here that I want to date and she won't date me, not while we're in danger." Roane kept his eyes steady on Ragen, his heart in them for her to read.

"That's a good question, Roane. I really don't know." John took back the letter, sealing it into an evidence bag that he pulled from his pocket. After initialing and dating it, he tucked it away. "I'm off. I'll be back. If you think of anything, either one of you, call me."

Ragen frowned as the door closed behind him before she turned to the two brothers, her frown deepening.

"So, how do we do this? I want this over and over yesterday." The men grinned at the fierceness of her voice and agreed with her. It needed to end and end that day.

Chapter 33

The next morning, Ragen walked through the down town area of the town, her hand tight in Roane's, his siblings walking in step with them. She was afraid but knew that she had taken her fear and terror to her Abba Father and that He had given her the peace that she needed for that day.

"Where are we eating. Roane?" Artis finally asked. They had agreed to go out for a meal, just to put themselves out there. The siblings had agreed that their girlfriends and boyfriends would meet them at a restaurant. That had not yet been determined.

"At the diner. Jake's set aside his party room for us and had agreed to let the others know to meet us there." Roane threw a grin at Artis who made a face back at him. The siblings were close and this with Roane had drawn them even closer. "Skyler and Slavin are joking us as is Nickol. I couldn't say no."

"No, it's okay, Roane. They are around enough to be considered honorary siblings." Arin shook her head at Ryley.

"And we will work on this at some point today?" Ragen had made that a condition of eating out, to go back to Roane's house and spend time working on it. But she knew him well enough to know that time would be spent in prayer before that happened.

"We will. For now, let's set it aside, love, and just enjoy a meal with this group." Roane grinned at her as the choruses from his siblings teased him.

———

Ragen stared up at him for a moment before she struggled to release her hand from his. She turned and walked away, leaving Roane staring after her, not moving to follow her. She needed to be away from him for a while, she decided, and think through what was happening. Ragen disappeared from sight before Roane could make a move.

His siblings stood nearby, their gaze shifting between Roane and where they had last seen Ragen. All were waiting for him to react but he didn't. Roane didn't move.

"Roane?" Ryley spoke at last, a question in his voice.

"I have to let her go, Ryley. If I don't, she'll resent me and then walk away from me. I don't want that." Roane's head tilted up even as his eyes closed against the raw emotions that he was feeling. He then turned and walked away, leaving the other four staring after him.

"He's right." Rowan spoke at last, reaching for the diner door. "Let's at least get a coffee and make some plans. We need to do that. I just don't know if we'll have a chance to put them into place."

Roane paced his house the next morning. He had heard no sound from the apartment and that worried him. It seemed as if Ragen had just disappeared on him. He finally turned to find his easy chair, his head bowing as he prayed through this situation. He knew that God was in control and would protect his lady. He just wanted to be the one to do that. Roane had been raised to take everything to his Abba Father and that was what he was struggling to do. His humanness wanted him out there to search for her.

Raising his head as he heard the doorbell, Roane sighed. He didn't want any company. It wasn't one of his siblings, he knew that. They each had keys to one another's homes and would just enter.

Starting at John and Peter, Roane finally moved back to let them enter. He headed for the kitchen, his mug of coffee refilled before he turned to face the men.

"What do you need, John?" Roane didn't hesitate to challenge his friend.

"Just to be with you. We're both off today. Rowan called last night." Peter spoke for the two men, his eyes assessing Roane and seeing the changes in his friend.

"I see. I would have called but Ragen needs this time to be on her own. She was likely feeling smothered and that we can't have." Roane drew a deep breath, his mouth opening to speak even as John shook his head.

"It's not that, Roane. She's running, in part to keep you safe. The word we're hearing from the street is that you're in danger. We're trying to track by whom but that's a difficult task at the moment."

"I know. We're working on that as well." His mug set on the counter, Roane walked out of the room to retrieve the copy of the paperwork that his family had sent to him. "Here. Take a look at this and tell me what you see. I know what I see and I don't like it one bit. My family's worried about me."

Peter moved to stand next to his cousin, reading the paperwork as well. John and Peter shared a look when they were done.

"How did they come up with this, Roane?" John just had to ask that question, knowing the family.

"I don't know, to tell you the truth. You would need to speak with Arin or Ryley. They're the ones who had been working this." Roane sighed, a deep from the toes sigh. "I want this over, John. How do we do that?"

"That's a good question, Roane. We're eliminating people from the suspect list, but more keep getting added. I don't know if you're aware that you have been targeted for years. We're only hearing that now."

"I see. And do you know by whom?" Roane watched as John hesitated before shaking his head. "About what I thought." He turned to stare out of the kitchen window. "I want this over, John. This is affecting my family as well as my livelihood. Is someone trying to discredit me?"

"That's part of what I'm hearing." Peter spoke up. "If they can discredit you, then any cases that you have worked on will be suspect. And if they have gone to court, then they can play it that you were incompetent."

Roane nodded. Peter was correct. It was what his father had spoken about with him the night before. Rourke was worried about that, knowing that Roane's reputation may well be destroyed. He was working with his lawyer friends to ensure that didn't happen.

"Dad mentioned that last night. I don't know what to say or do."

The two men finally left, not satisfied that they had made any progress in the investigation. Roane locked the door behind them, his hand resting against the closed door before he was reaching for his shoes and running for his car, heading for the downtown area. Surely, he thought, someone has seen Ragen.

Chapter 34

Tucking what she had purchased at the second-hand store into her backpack, Ragen drew a deep breath. She needed to go back to her home. Only, she wasn't sure how to do that. Roane would be looking for her, she was well aware of that. Ragen was trying her best to avoid him, knowing that he was in danger because of her. The cruel and vicious letter that had appeared on her door the day that she had run stated that. She just didn't know why. Ragen had stared at it before she just dropped it to the tabletop and walked away. She had not let anyone know of the letter, thinking that if she ignored it, it would go away.

Walking rapidly away from the store, Ragen searched for somewhere that she could hide until she decided what to do. A woman from the street reached out to her, drawing her to one side.

"You're looking for somewhere to hide?" The woman, around Ragen's own age, had nodded.

"I am. But how did you know?" Ragen was puzzled by that.

"Because I have seen you with Roane. Roane and his family are good support for those of us who are down on our luck and on the street for a while. We watch out for them and their families. Come on. I'll show where I stay. It's safe and hidden away from sight." The woman stared around before she drew Ragen with her. "I'm Annie. And you are Ragen." She gave another grin as Ragen stared at her. "We know your name, Ragen. It's how we look after that family."

Ragen had shrugged, not sure if she should trust the woman. God was not stopping her from going with her, that she sensed. She stared around at the room in the abandoned building, thinking that it was comfortable. It didn't appear to be part of the abandoned building but something one would find in a home. What she didn't know was that Annie was an undercover officer, ready to come in from the streets. For now, Annie was delegated to watch over Ragen.

A week passed with Ragen hiding on the streets, accompanied by Annie or other of Annie's friends. Ragen wondered at that, not realizing that they were protecting her. Men had taken to the streets, searching for her and her new friends were doing what they could to hide her.

Annie turned to Ragen at the week's mark, searching her face. She shook her head. Ragen was hurting in many ways, and there didn't seem to be an end to what she was facing.

"Ragen? What can we do for you? You're running and hiding but that doesn't help to end whatever it is you are facing." Annie had drawn Ragen down to a bench in the downtown area of the town.

"No, it doesn't. I don't know what to do, Annie. To tell you the truth, I want to go back to my home but I don't know how safe that would be. And I want to see Roane but I think that would be too dangerous." Ragen didn't look up as she focused on the ground in front of her. She didn't hear the soft exclamation from the man who had stopped there.

Peter sat beside Ragen, a glance shared with Annie. Annie had reached out to him, knowing that Ragen wouldn't survive much longer on the streets. Her beauty was striking and that made her stand out.

"Peter?" Annie's voice shook Ragen and had her looking up and then to her side.

Ragen sighed. Peter just had to show up, didn't he?

"Peter? Why are you here?" Ragen didn't wait for him to respond, instead rising to her feet and almost running from him.

Peter stood, watching as she ran, not sure where she would end up.

"Annie?" His quiet question didn't ask much but Annie understood.

"She's running, Peter, and trying to keep herself safe as well as keeping Roane safe. Unfortunately, it's not working out as she thought it would. And I have no idea where she'll end up. She wants to go back to her own home."

"I can understand that." Peter sat back down, a frown on his face as he thought through what he knew. "We need to find her, Annie."

"I know, but we won't. She'll hide and that makes it more dangerous for her." Annie was on her feet, heading in the direction that Ragen had run to, knowing that she wouldn't find the other lady.

Ragen Found a sheltered bench in the grove of trees that made up a portion of the downtown area. She sat, her eyes closing. She was exhausted and knew that she could not continue to run. It was only wearing her out and causing more worry for Roane. Ragen decided at that point that she would go on the offensive, even if it meant her life. This had to end.

With that thought, Ragen just bowed her head and began to pray, begging God to protect her and bring a resolution to whatever this was that she was involved in. Her mind stilled as she waited for Him, feeling His peace working in her heart. She thought of the verses of peace, protection and joy that she had memorized over the years. That would be what would get her through.

Not hearing the footsteps that had approached her, Ragen jumped as she felt someone sit beside her. She refused to look up, afraid that it would be someone meaning her harm. Instead, she felt an arm around her, drawing her close to the man who sat there. She sighed as she heard Roane's voice. Somehow, he had found her. That was not what she had planned on but it seemed as if God had.

"Ragen? Will you come home?" Roane didn't push her, instead waiting patiently for her to react. He would wait as long as it took for that to happen.

Ragen finally nodded. She had to, she decided, go home to the apartment until this was all over and then she would move on, leaving her heard behind.

"I will, Roane. I'm sorry. I needed some time." Ragen sniffed, her emotions raw at the moment.

"I know, sweetheart. I know. You need to take back your life and find that joy that you had before once more. Let me help you." Roane was on his feet, his hand held out for Ragen to take.

Ragen studied Roane's hand, knowing that once she took it, she would never walk away from him again. She suspected that he had feelings for her but it was in God's timing if they ever acted on them.

Ragen watched Roane closely as he searched through the paperwork stacked on his desk. She sighed before she reached to help him, sorting it out for him. Roane had stared at her for a moment before he grinned at her. They made a good team, he decided.

"Roane? What were you looking for? Or rather who?" Ragen looked up at that point, catching a look in Roane's eyes that said he cherished her.

"What was I looking for?" He reached for the paperwork, reading through it. "This is Rowan's work. I'm not sure what he was looking for." He turned as he heard a voice calling for him. "John? You're here?"

"I am, Roane. I've been told to work with you for now. We need to solve this. The ramifications of what you are facing are just growing." John hadn't wanted to come, to tell his friend that it was much deeper than they had ever thought.

"What do you mean?" Roane reached to wrap Ragen tight to him, afraid for his lady.

"That there are more people involved that we thought." John held up a folder. "This is what I can share with you. But first, we need to pray. I understand that your family is heading this was with their significant others and also Peter and his team will be here. Also, Abe, Richard, and Don are moving in. Emma has forwarded information to you, she tells me, that you need to look at."

Roane nodded. He was familiar with the names, meeting them when his friends had gone through what they had.

"That's good, I think. I don't have a lot of room though." Roane looked around, seeing the smile that Ragen was trying to hide. "You think this is funny?"

"I do. You're usually calm and collected and organized. You're not right now and we need to do that." Ragen walked away, hearing the ladies' voices from the kitchen, hugging the men as they passed her, heading for the office and looking for their son and brother.

John gave a low laugh. It was not often that Roane was put on the spot like that.

"She has your number, you know, Roane." John looked around as the room suddenly seemed full. "I see that we are all here. Let's find the ladies and spend time in prayer." He walked away, leaving Roane staring down at the floor.

Rourke reached to wrap an arm around his son's shoulder, praying for him as he did so.

"Where did you find Ragen?"

"Downtown, Dad. She was just sitting on a park bench. I am so afraid for her. I can't lose her." Roane blinked back tears, trying to control his emotions.

"She has your heart, son. Don't say anything. She needs to hear that from you, if you can ever tell her that." Rourke nudged his son forward. "Let's find the others and spend that time in prayer. This is when it gets so dangerous for you both."

"It does, Dad. I just don't understand it." Roane's feet stopped moving suddenly as he paled.

"Son? What did you just think of?" Rourke waited patiently for Roane to speak, shaking his head at his wife.

"I know who it is. God help us. I don't know that we'll survive." Roane had trouble keeping on his feet, his father's hand on his arm seeming to be the only thing keeping him upright.

"Roane? Who?" Rourke almost shook his son to get him to answer. "Who is it?"

Roane uttered a name, a name familiar to his father. Rourke stared at him, his face paling as he thought through what he knew.

"Of course. He had contacts in Ragen's town. We always wondered how he made his money. His parents didn't have it, working pay cheque to pay cheque. We'll find that information, son, and bring him down. God will protect us. We may not like what we face but we will face him and be victorious. We will find that joy in living that we seemed to have set aside for now."

"Thanks, Dad." Roane had his eyes on his mother. "Mom?"

Sofi reached to hug her son, knowing that he was highly disturbed. She couldn't fix this for him, not this time, not like when he had been young.

"I agree with you, son. He has always been skirting the edge of lawfulness. As your father has stated, we pray and then we work through this." She turned slightly as she felt a presence beside her. "Ragen? You've come to find Roane?" At Ragen's nod, Sofi turned back to Roane. "Roane, bring your lady with you. We're arming ourselves for this fight." She walked away, leaving Ragen staring after her.

"Mom's right, Ragen. You are my lady. And we do need to arm ourselves for this fight." Roane dropped a kiss on Ragen's temple. "Let's find our prayer group and then get to work."

Four hours later, John rose from where he had been sitting, needing to move around. He thought best sometimes when he was pacing. Moving through the house to the outdoors, he contemplated the names and information that they had accrued over the hours, highly disturbed that this information had not been available sooner. Perhaps, John thought, Roane and Ragen would not have gone through what they had.

"It would have happened anyway." Abe paced beside John, Richard and Don with them. Peter stood where he could watch them and the backyard.

"It likely would have. I just wish that it had been different." John stopped, his face tilting to let the sun warm it.

"It's how it always is, John. You know that. We've all experienced it." Richard spoke for the three security team heads that had had what was termed as adventures. "No matter how much we would have wanted to change things, God led us through and used us to bring people to justice."

"He did at that." Don agreed. He pointed back towards the house. "We now have to come up with a plan to bring that man and his cronies to justice. If we don't, Ragen will be out there on her own and trying to do that. That would certainly mean harm or even death for her.

———

The very next day, Ragen was doing just that, putting herself out. She walked the downtown area, knowing that she was being followed and for the moment not caring. She had walked away from Roane that morning, shaking her head. Roane had work that he needed to do, she knew, and just couldn't be with her.

John watched Ragen for a moment before he walked up to her, standing in front of her and causing her to stop. He gave a brief grin at the look that she threw at him.

"Escaping, Ragen?" His grin widened as she glared at him. "How be we have a coffee and you can let me know your plans."

Ragen sighed. John just had to be there, didn't he? She didn't want to have coffee with him but it seemed as if she could not avoid that.

"Okay, I guess. Just tell me what you want to ask me now." Ragen slid on the booth seat, a nod at the server.

"First, let me pray with you. I do have some questions for you about your hometown." John waited for their coffees to be set in front of him. "Talk to me, Ragen. Tell me about your town."

"What do you want to know? It was small and tight-knit, I guess that you could say. I didn't really fit in with them. There was always a sense that I felt of

———

something wrong, that someone was pulling the strings. Does that make sense?"

"It does, given what we have discovered so far. What we said yesterday about things reaching to your town? It has been confirmed." John sighed to himself. This was not going to be easy. "I found out that your paternal grandfather was involved."

"He was? I never knew him." Ragen studied the tabletop in front of her. "How?"

"We're working through it all. He seems to have been a contact for those wanting to hide from the law."

Ragen nodded. There had been rumours of that over the years but she had ignored them.

"I had heard of that but ignored it. I guess that I shouldn't have."

"There was nothing confirmed, Ragen. You were young and likely just put it off as rumours. Now, if you can write down anything that might help us, I would appreciate it." John was on his feet as Ragen slid from the booth. "Did you walk?"

"I did. I don't have a car." Ragen paused for a moment, feeling a sense of great evil near her. She could only beg God to remove it. "And you're going to drive me home, aren't you?"

"That's my intention, Ragen." John tucked her into his police car, pausing to look around. He could feel himself watched and he too felt the sense of grave danger approaching them.

Roane paced his front porch, glancing frequently at his watch. Ragen had been gone for over two hours.

———

He ran for his car, heading for the downtown area, surprised to see streets blocked off. Out of his car, he headed for the police tape, surprised to find Peter waiting there.

"Peter? What's going on?" Roane's voice had Peter glancing at him.

"John. They found his car but not him. And the server at the diner said that Ragen was with him. She's missing as well." Peter was worried for his cousin. He was all too familiar with what could happen to an officer.

"What?" Roane's voice sounded too loud in the silence around him. He scrubbed at his face. "Ragen walked downtown today. She needed to do that, she said, and wouldn't let me go with her. I had an investigation that I had to finish." Roane paced, a hand rubbing at his cheek still. "Who? And where?"

Peter nodded. Roane had gone right to the centre of the problem. He reached for Roane's arm, pulling him back to his vehicle.

"We need to search, Roane. Only I have no idea where to start." Peter knew that his team was around them, watching for anyone after Roane. "This was done to get to you, I think, Roane."

Roane nodded, having come to that conclusion himself. He had no idea who was after him, or did he? He frowned at Peter, knowing that the man with him would not leave the area willingly, not while his cousin was missing.

"Peter? What can we do? How do we search this through?" Roane sighed. "Emma was to call this afternoon. I don't know what to tell her."

"She'll already know, Roane. She seems to be able to sense when something bad has happened to a friend. Emma can't explain it, simply stating that it is God at work in her that does that."

"That's what Abe has said." Roane became more worried as each moment passed. "Where do we even start to look for them?"

"That a good question." Jerome stood beside him, Edward behind him. The two officers had found Roane and knew that he was at risk of disappearing as well. "We need to get you out of sight, Roane, and keep you that way. This is likely directed at you."

"But you don't know that for sure, do you?" Roane was challenging Jerome and they both knew it. He turned and walked away, finding his father and Rowan waiting for him. Rourke reached for his car keys, pointing that way.

Jerome and Edward watched as the three men walked away before turning to watch Peter.

"Peter? What are your thoughts?" Edward shared a look with Jerome before he turned slowly in a circle, studying the crowd that had gathered.

"I really don't know. I had a text message from John about two hours ago, just stating that he had Ragen with him and was heading back to his office. Obviously,, he didn't make it."

"No, he didn't. And I want to know why and who." Jerome blew out a breath. Those were questions that would need to wait for an answer, an answer that wouldn't come for days. He feared for his friend and fellow office. Edward walked away, mingling with the crowd and Jerome watched. Someone out there knew what had happened but would they come forward? That was a question that they had never expected to ask about John. He was too good and too careful of an officer to disappear this way.

Chapter 36

A day passed. Then a second day without anyone knowing either John or Ragen were or if they were still alive. They were all out there searching, his fellow officers whether on duty or off. The other emergency services were the same. The undercover officers were searching hourly in the abandoned buildings as were the people on the street. There was just no sign of either John or Ragen. Concern and fear was growing hourly for their safety.

Roane and his family were searching the streets and abandoned building as well. His father and brothers were searching the internet for anywhere that they could find them. That just wasn't happening. Abe and Emma had appeared on the second day, settling down to work with the family. Abe's team, Richard's team, Don, another friend with a security team, and then Peter's own team were out there, canvassing wherever it was that they could.

On the third day, Edward walked slowly back towards his patrol vehicle. His steps were slow and weighted. He was more than a little worried about his friend and his other friend's lady. Just where were they? Edward had to acknowledge that God was in control and that everything that was taken place was under His hand. It just didn't make it any easier.

His steps hesitated and then Edward stopped walking, his eyes on the paper bag that sat on the hood of his car. He looked around, not seeing anyone but feeling himself watched. He had no idea what it might contain.   Approaching it carefully, Edward still hesitated before he reached to unroll the top of the bag and then cautiously open it. He frowned as he stared down into it. A police issue resolver, he recognized, and then he saw the police shield, positioned in such a way to show the officer's badge number. Edward drew in a deep breath before he was turning in a circle, studying the area around him. It was in the suburbs and he had answered a call about a nuisance neighbour. He now wondered if that had been a setup. Edward reached for the bag and hurriedly found his seat behind the steering wheel. He still waited for a moment before he drove off, not seeing the youth who appeared at the edge of a lawn, watching him and knowing that he had done the best that he could to alert the officers that their friend and fellow officer was still alive. He just didn't know where he or Ragen were now. They had been moved in the early morning hours, leaving that evidence behind them.

Jerome looked up at the tap at his office door, sitting back in his chair and beckoning Edward in to the room. He frowned at the bag that Edward set carefully on his desk.

"Edward? What is this?" Jerome reached for it, opening it in shock and then dumping it out. "These are John's?"

"The shield is. I suspect the weapon is as well. We'll need to verify that." Edward slumped into a chair, his hands rubbing at his face. "I didn't see who left it. And the dash cam doesn't show anything too clearly. Whoever it was moved in and out very quickly. I think it was someone young but I'm not sure. I've asked the crime lab to take a look at it."

Edward nodded, his thoughts not on what Edward was saying.

"We don't know if he's still alive or not, do we?" That frustrated both men. "And now we have to search even harder. Who knows what the two are facing."

"Or even if they are still in town." Edward didn't look up but heard the soft sound of agreement from Jerome. "We'll need to reach out to Peter."

"And we will. Where were you?"

Edward looked up at that point, nodded, and then explained just where he was. Jerome's eyes never left his face. When Edward was finished, Jerome reached for his computer keyboard, keying in the address and then reading the information. "That house you were parked in front of? It belongs to the mayor's son."

"And he has been rumoured for years to be on the wrong side of the law." Edward blew out a breath of frustration. "We'll need to investigate him but keep it very quiet."

"I agree." Jerome reached to send off an email. "I'll ask Emma to search it. And then we'll verify what she finds."

"That we will. Where do you want me, Jerome? I'm off duty now." Edward drew in a deep breath. "Do we even know where to search?"

Jerome shook his head, his eyes on the officer hesitating outside of his door. "Angie?"

———

"Jerome? We just had word that John and Ragen were seen earlier today. In Roane's neighbourhood. We can't confirm just where though. And so far,, we have to treat it as a rumour or tip that we need to investigate."

"We do." Jerome turned to Edward. "Go with Angie, Edward." He was on his own feet, heading for the supervisor on duty and Edward's own supervisor. "I'll see about authorizing overtime for you."

Edward gave a brief nod before he was out of the department door and then fastening his seatbelt in Angie's car.

"Do you think this is true or just another false trail?" Edward's voice held hope as he searched the area around them.

"I pray that it's true, Edward. We need to find them. They are both missed." Angie drove slowly through Roane's neighbourhood. "How well do you know his neighbours?"

"Not that well." Edward reached to unfasten his seatbelt, watching the movement in the neighbourhood. "Roane will be out here as soon as he realizes we are."

"No. I put in a call to Peter and then Rowan. They'll keep him inside, as difficult as that might be." Angie walked towards the first house, Edward's steps in time with hers.

Two hours later, they both slumped in the car seats, looking at one another. They had not accomplished anything, they decided. There was just no way that John and Ragen had been there, not from what they were told. Yet their instincts honed on the streets were telling them that the two had been there at some point over the last couple of days.

"Where now, Angie? I don't think we'll getting any further ahead." Edward was frustrated at that as he knew everyone else was. "There's someone out there, someone watching us."

"There is. I feel the evil surrounding us. Only God is going to keep them safe and bring them home." Angie drew in a deep breath. "Are the families prepared for how they might come home?"

Edward shook his head. He had no idea if they were prepared to hold a funeral of either one of the two. He just prayed that this would not be the case.

Chapter 37

The day that John and Ragen disappeared the week before, John had held the door for Ragen to exit the restaurant and then with a hand to her lower back, rushed her towards his car. He felt the evil approaching them and wanted to get her away from that area. He was praying hard that he could. Only it didn't work out that way. He heard a scream from Ragen before he was facedown on the ground, the force with which he was struck taking his breath away for a moment. John vaguely felt his handcuffs clicking around his wrists before he was pulled to his feet. His vision was blurry and he could only faintly hear the sounds around him. His weapon and police shield were pulled from his belt and tossed to one side to one of the men who tucked them away into a pocket before he was shoved almost violently into the car.

Ragen struggled with the man who had her wrist in his hard grasp without being able to free herself and flee from there. She spun on the car seat to stare at John, knowing that he would not be able to help them escape. Shoved back against the seat and a belt strapped around her, Ragen continued to fight until she saw the weapon appear in the man's hand, directed not at herself but at John. John was seated beside her, his head back and his eyes closed. Ragen knew that he was hurting, She just didn't know how bad it was.

Her eyes searched the men in the car, her fear growing with each breath that she took. She prayed for release, knowing that wouldn't likely happen. How

---

could she get away and get John away as well? That was something Ragen was desperately searching for answers to. Only there were no answers.

The car pulled into a garage and then stopped, the garage door lowering behind them. Ragen had not watched the area, not realizing how close to home and Roane that she was. Just down the street in fact. She was viciously pulled from the car, the man not caring that her head hit the door frame as she exited it. She could hear John's faltering steps as he too was pulled from the car and then shoved towards the house door.

Once inside, a hand was kept clamped on Ragen's arm until she was pulled down the hallway and shoved into a room, the door slamming behind her and locked. She ran for it, tugging at the door knob and then running around the room, searching for a way out or for something to use to protect her. Nothing was there. Back at the door, Ragen could hear John's steps passing her door and then the door next to her slamming shut. She begging God to release John and let him go back to his family and friends. She didn't care about herself at that point.

Neither of the captives were provided with any food or drinks of any kind. All they had was the water that they could find in the small ensuites in each of their rooms. John paced that night, desperate to find a way to get out and not doing so. His head was clearing to some degree but he had no idea who had taken him and Ragen captive. John had felt along his belt for his weapon and shield, dismayed that they had disappeared. That was not what he wanted to discover.

———

His phone was also missing, where it was, he had no idea.

On the third day, their doors were unlocked and men approached them. Ragen gave a small scream as a blindfold was dropped over her eyes before she was hauled in a rough manner from the room and out to a car again. She could sense that someone was beside her, her arm rubbing against the man. She prayed that it was John, that he was not seriously hurt. Ragen tried to follow the twists and turns that the vehicle made but she was soon lost to that. Her mind instead turned to Roane and his family and she begged God to protect them and keep them from harm. She prayed for John, that he would be released. For herself? She prayed that her death would be easy and not prolonged. She doubted that she would ever be free.

The two were pulled from the car again and once more walked into a building, hands on their arms directing where they walked to. Shoved into rooms separately again, they both stumbled at the viciousness of the shoves, barely able to stand.

John waited for how long he was never sure before he raised his hands, the handcuffs still on his wrists and pulled the blindfold from his eyes. He blinked, his eyes squinting in the dim light. He stared around before he was searching for a way out or a way to reach Ragen. John couldn't find any way out of the room aside from the locked door. The windows were too high for him to reach. His thoughts turned to Ragen and he began to pray for her.

A week after their disappearance, Jerome looked up as he heard almost running steps approaching the conference room that he was working in. He stared at Edward as that office slid to a halt near him.

"Edward?" The question lingered in the air that Jerome would not or could not ask.

"We found them. Daniel has gone for the search warrants." Edward drew in a deep breath. "They're near where Rourke had his office."

"That close? Rourke wondered that." Jerome looked down at what he was working on before he gathered in together and almost ran to lock it into his office before heading for his car, Edward keeping close steps with him.

The officers gathered outside of the mansion, mingling for a moment before Jerome called them together, setting out what duties that they each had. The emergency task force officers were geared up, ready to enter first. Jerome frowned. There just didn't seem to be any activity around the building.

"We're sure on this, Daniel?" Jerome rubbed at his cheek, still not certain that they had the right building.

"We are. A source came through this morning. That person said there are no other people there other than John and Ragen. He didn't want to go in, not by himself. He's somewhat afraid of the building owner." Daniel was frustrated at that but could understand the man's hesitation to some extent.

"Okay, let's do this." Jerome walked towards the building, following the officers already at the door.

Officers ran towards the building, heading to search. Stopped by two padlocked doors, they exchanged looks before the doors were broken down and they were inside, searching for the two and finding them.

Chapter 38

Edward dropped to his knees beside John, a hand on his friend's wrist. A sound from a follow officer had him looking up.

"He's alive but in rough shape. Here. Help me get him to his feet." Edward's arm was around his friend and fellow officer as he pulled one of John's arms around his shoulder. The officer on John's other side did the same before they began a slow hesitant walk to the outdoors. Edward glanced towards the other room, hearing Jerome's low voice before his concentration went back to John.

Finding the paramedics waiting for them, Edward stepped back as John sank down onto the stretcher, his eyes closing once more. He waited for a few moments before he turned, not sure where he needed to be or where he should be.

"Edward? Who's riding with John?" Angie had found him, sent that way by Jerome. "Jerome wants you to."

Edward glanced back towards the ambulance before he nodded.

"I can do that. I came with someone else." He turned to walk towards where the ambulance was preparing to depart, climbing in and finding his seat. All he could do at the present time was pray for his friend and fellow officer. Not one of them knew what had happened to John over the past seven days but it was drastic, that much was obvious.

———

Jerome stood for a moment, watching as paramedics worked on Ragen before he turned to find Angie, stepping from the room. He glanced back as well to where John had been hidden away. That was it, he decided. They had been hidden away, not meant to be found at all.

"Jerome?" Angie stood waiting for him. "How is Ragen?"

Jerome shrugged, not sure how to even answer that.

"I'm not sure, Angie. She's still out of it. She didn't even move when we removed the handcuffs. Listen. Find a female officer to go with her. You've got the scene here, right?" At her nod, Jerome paused again, not sure where he needed to be. "I need to find Roane and his family. He needs to be there for Ragen. As far as we know, she has no next of kin but it seems as if they are moving that way towards one another."

Angie gave a quick grin. She was friends with Arin and those two ladies had discussed that between themselves.

"I can see that. Roane has never acted towards another lady as he is towards Ragen. Go. Do what you need to do. Catch up with me later. Although I don't think we'll be here long, given the lack of evidence that we can see." Angie walked away, leaving Jerome staring down at the keys now in his hand.

Roane turned from his door, letting Jerome in before he headed once more for his office. His steps slowed as Jerome spoke. He spun to stare at his friend, finding his father and mother now flanking him.

"What was that you said, Jerome?" Roane walked back to stand in front of his friend. "I thought you said that you had found Ragen."

"We have both Ragen and John, Roane. They are likely both at the hospital by now." Jerome watched with compassion as Roane's eyes slid closed and then popped back open.

"What did they say?" When Jerome didn't answer, Roane stepped closer. "What did they say?"

"Nothing as yet. They're both unconscious. Come on. Let's get you to your lady. You need to be there as her next of kin." Jerome's eyes lifted to watch his friend's parents, a couple he considered friends. "Rourke? Sofi?"

"Go on with Jerome, son. We'll lock up and follow you." Rourke reached to hug his son, his father prayer whispering in his son's ear.

Pacing the waiting room in the Emergency Department, Roane kept glancing at the door to the examination area. He wanted to find his lady, who he admitted to himself finally that he loved deeply. He didn't want to lose her. He needed to talk to her, to find out her feelings and whether she loved him or not. Roane turned as he felt an arm around him. Artis stood beside him, her eyes on her brother. He was hurting and she couldn't make it better for him.

"Roane? Any word?" Artis' voice was barely audible in the bustle and noise of the room.

Roane shook his head, reaching to hug his sister. His eyes found the rest of his family, the ladies seated and the men standing to protect them from curious eyes. He saw Peter and his team around them as well and was grateful for that.

"No yet. Jerome is back there or he was. I'm not sure what is happening." Roane swiped at his eyes, the tears that he refused to shed clouding them for a moment.. "Have you heard anything on John?"

Artis shook her head, stepping to one side as Peter approached, having heard Roane's question.

"The medical professionals are with him right now, Roane. We haven't heard anything as yet but we should shortly." Peter turned as someone touched his arm, moving off with the nurse and towards his cousin.

"He's had word, hasn't he?" Roane was growing angry, not at Peter, not at the medical staff but at what had happened. He had kept those feelings tamped down until now. He had difficulty controlling his emotions, spinning and almost running from the room to begin to pace in the parking lot, not realizing that his two brothers flanked him and that multiple officers were around him as well. This would be a perfect opportunity for Roane to disappear.

Rowan watched the men at the edge of the parking lot whose attention seemed to be solely on Roane. He nodded to himself as officers moved in on them and then moved them away, shoving them into a patrol vehicle. Ryley exchanged a look with his brother before his eyes settled back on Roane. Neither brother could begin to understand the emotions that were roiling inside their brother and now showing on

his face and in his eyes. Roane needed to see Ragen
and for now, that was not possible.

Chapter 39

An hour later, Peter stood at his cousin's bedside, frowning down at John. John had not roused and that was concerning them all. Until they knew exactly what had transpired over the week, they could not move forward with any arrests. He didn't hear the sounds around him, concentrating as he was on John. Peter turned as he felt a hand on his shoulder. Rourke stood there, his eyes closed as he prayed for his young friends.

"What's the word, Peter?" Rourke eyed first Peter and then John.

"They haven't really said. I don't know that they know much about what went on. John has not awakened but they were not too surprised at that. It does concern them. They're thinking that he hasn't eaten or had much to drink during the last week. That's how they're reading it." Peter was frustrated to say the least. He acknowledged that God was in control but that didn't make him feel better at this point. Peter would need to have that out with God at some point over the next few hours. "How's Ragen?"

"About the same. She did rouse somewhat when Roane found her and was able to give something of a statement to Jerome. She doesn't know much though about who held them or why." Rourke was worried about John and Ragen. Roane's heart was involved with Ragen, he knew that much. "Let me pray with you. Your wife is in the waiting room with your kids. She asked that I let you know. John's people still

---

haven't been found where they are out in the woods of the north."

"No, I didn't think that they would be. They can't be when they're out there. The only way in is by float plane and then walking. I don't know how else to reach them." Peter was worried.

"Jerome was speaking with someone, he said, to see what they could do." Rourke's hand returned to rest on Peter's shoulder even as his other hand rested on John's arm before his head was bent and he was praying for the two younger men, begging God almost to resolve this and return John and Ragen to full health. He just didn't put into words what they were all thinking, that the two would not be the same after this.`

The next day, John was still lying unconscious, not aware of who was around him. He didn't feel his mother's hand on his hair or hear his father's prayer for his son. Jerome had succeeded in tracking them down, and the pilot from the Barnabas Foundation had headed to bring them home. Barnabas had not hesitated at all to offer their assistance.

Roane refused to leave Ragen, working as he could on his laptop, his brothers and sisters bringing him what he needed. Rourke had stood and watched his son, praying for peace in the situation for the couple and also for them to find joy once it was all over. He knew only too well how hard it was to find joy in the circumstances even though it was possible.

Ragen had roused, not sure where she was. She could feel a hand on hers and wondered at that. She felt safe and warm but could not understand that. Her eyes opened just a crack as she looked around before they opened totally in surprise. Ragen could hear someone speaking from beside her but for the moment, she was just too taken up with the fact that she seemed to be free. She finally turned to the form standing beside her.

"Ragen!" Roane's voice was full of joy and the love that he felt for her. "You're awake. Welcome home, darling."

Ragen frowned at him, swallowing hard to try and lubricate her throat.

"Roane?" Her voice was a mere weak whisper. "Where am I?"

"You're in our hospital, darling, and safe. Jerome and Peter have made sure of that." Roane tilted his head to study her before he gave into an impulse and simply bent over to kiss her, a hand resting on her cheek. "I thought that I had lost you forever. God was good, darling. He brought you home."

"Is this what it is, Roane? Home?" Ragen licked at her dry lips, her heart praising God that He had heard her pleas for release. "John?"

"He's safe too. They found you two yesterday and brought you home." Roane's hand tightened on Ragen's. "You'll need to give your statement." He looked around as he heard footsteps. "And here is Jerome."

"Don't leave me, Roane. Please don't leave me." Ragen was in tears at the thought of Roane walking away from her. "I won't say anything if you're not here. Jerome?"

Jerome finally nodded, seeing the agitation and fear that was growing in her.

"For now, Roane can stay. Talk to me, Ragen. Tell me what happened." Jerome's notepad and pen were out.

"I can't say much. I never say the men. Never saw the outside of where we were kept. All I know is that John and I were in separate rooms. We were not asked for anything or told to do anything." Ragen frowned at Jerome. "We weren't given any food and only minimal water. Except for the last two days. We weren't given anything. I think that they wanted us to die." Ragen's eyes closed as she struggled with her emotions and the tears that just would not stop.

Jerome nodded. John had been awake briefly and gave much of the same statement. Angie was hard at work and digging into who owned the house where they were found. She simply told him that she was on the line of who it was and that he was not going to like what she was finding. Jerome had stared at her, opened his mouth to ask her a question and then snapped it closed. He walked away, discouraged for the time being.

"John has said the same. He was puzzled by that." Jerome watched as Ragen simply slept, her body not letting her stay awake any longer.

"Jerome? Where exactly do we stand with the investigation? And do we know who or why?" Roane was not backing down, not this time. His lady had been harmed as had been a good friend.

"We are trying our best, Roane. You know how it works." Jerome spat out his words, not angry at Roane but at the situation that they faced. "We are getting there. Angie has a line on who and why. We just need a couple of days."

"And will we still be alive at that point?" Roane didn't look at Jerome, didn't see him stare at Roane before he walked away, nodding at Peter as he did so.

Chapter 40

Two days later, Roane stood where he could watch Ragen. She had curled up in a recliner in his parents' living room, seeming to be asleep, but he doubted that. It was more likely, he decided, that she was trying to heal and didn't want to speak with any one. His attention then went to John, who had stretched out on the couch. He was asleep, Roane knew, his exhaustion evident to all of them. John's parents were around the house somewhere, he was well aware of that. Jerome had insisted that the two and their families be in one house just so tht they would protect them better.

Peter and his team were inside the house. Peter had called in two other teams, Richard and Don, to help with outside security. They would work it out between them when and where they were stationed. Another friend, Abe, had his team in town, staking out a house where the mastermind to this all had been found. They would not move away from it unless that man did. Jerome had sent in officers to be with them, well aware that Abe's team was likely better trained and more experienced that the officers attached with them.

Roane turned slightly as Ryley stopped beside him, an arm across his brother's shoulder. He didn't say anything, praying silently for his brother. He couldn't fathom how Roane was still on his feet and functioning.

"Ryley? What did you discover?" Roane spoke quietly, not wanting to disturb anyone around them.

His siblings were there, their boyfriends girlfriends there as well.

"Something that is puzzling all of us. How well do you know Trevor Smith?" Ryley didn't look at his brother but felt him stiffen.

"Him? He's behind this?" Roane shook his head. "That doesn't surprise me. He's had it in for me since we were in grade one. We could never understand why though."

"Jealousy for part. He's from what was termed the wrong side of town." Ryley looked up, praying for the words that he needed. "He hasn't changed, Roane. He still wants a piece of you. And we're not sure why. Emma has been shooting us information and we need you to look at it." He looked towards Ragen. "And it involves Ragen. Somehow he connected with her a few years ago. Emma states that he is the one who brought her to that town and then contacted you to find her. She's been able to trace everything back to him. Jerome has been copied with that information."

Roane stood silently, digesting Ryley's words before he walked towards his father's office, finding as he suspected his siblings and father and John's father there, working away. He reached for the paperwork being handed him and found a seat on the floor in a corner of the room, reading through it multiple times before he just sat, his hands resting on the papers on his legs. His eyes closed as he prayed, begging God for this to be over that day and that he could then move on with Ragen, choosing joy as a way of life instead of fear.

Ragen had roused at one point, her eyes opening as she searched the room, relief pouring through her as she recognized that she was as safe as she could be. She was on her feet, searching for Roane, sitting beside him as close as she could. His arm had come around her and drew her closer to him without his being aware of what he had done.

The families watched the couple before they shared looks and then went back to their study of the information. They were all determined to find what they could and then let Jerome or Angie have it. Angie had appeared at one point, taking what had been given her, checking on John and Ragen, and then leaving, heading for the office and the team working feverishly to finish the work that was needed. Arrest and search warrants were being obtained, the plans being to serve them that evening.

Jerome stood in front of the house that had been monitored all that day. Abe stood beside him, his attention not on Jerome or the house but on the surroundings. This is when it became dangerous for the officers.

"He's inside. He hasn't left in the last three days." Abe's voice was quiet and factual. Both men could hear the early evening sounds of nature and town life.

"We didn't think that he would. Thanks, Abe, for stepping in once more. The support and assistance of your three teams has been a relief for us as we worked through this." Jerome turned as he sensed someone beside him. Only no one was there. He looked up, knowing that God was present with him and that Jerome didn't need to fear what was coming next.

Jerome paced through the house, heading towards where he heard raised voices. He noted the number of both men and women already in handcuffs and being led from that house. He shook his head. Hopefully, Jerome prayed, this would end it all today. Roane and Ragen needed that.

Pausing in a doorway, Jerome studied the room before his eyes landed on the man, around his own age, who stood, shaking with rage. He was loudly protesting his arrest and what he called an invasion of his home and privacy. That man's anger turned on Jerome as he approached.

"What is the meaning of this? Just who do you think you are to come into my home and arrest my friends and employees?" Smith tried hard to escape the hands holding him, to charge towards Jerome.

Jerome simply held up the arrest warrants and search warrants.

"These say differently, Smith. The judge agreed with us when we approached him with our documentation and proof. Take him away." Jerome stepped to one side to watch as Smith was led away, still spouting hatred and defiance before he turned to start his search.

Angie walked towards him hours later as he stood in the break room at the department, fatigue drawing him down.

———

"Jerome?" Angie waited for Jerome to turn, seeing that he was as exhausted as she was. "We have them all. It was far worse than we thought."

"That's what we figured. You've done good work today, Angie. I'm glad that you're on our side. Are you at a point when you can leave it for the night?" Jerome knew that he was not making it home, the couch in his office being his bed that night.

"I am. I just wanted to find you and let you know that Smith's lawyers are not returning his calls. He has no lawyer." Angie gave a tired smile. "It's fitting, you know. He tried to alienate so many from their family and friends and ruin their lives. It worked with some but not others. Now, that has come full circle. No one wants anything to do with him. His friends and employees are talking as fast as we can interview them. He'll be going away for a long time. I doubt there will be a plea bargain offered to him."

"I don't think so either. Have a good night, Angie." Jerome retrieved his cup of coffee and headed for his office, sitting on the couch before he stretched out, asleep before he even was fully settled. It was over for John and also Roane and Ragen. He hadn't thought that it would involve what it had.

Chapter 41

Roane looked up two days later, finding Ragen standing beside him, her hand on his shoulder. He swept an arms around her and pulled her close, his eyes not leaving her face. He sensed that she had come to a conclusion. She had that look of peace and yes joy around her.

"Darling?" He whispered the endearment, afraid that she would walk away from him.

"Jerome's here. So is everyone else who can be. Your dad and brothers are working from here today, they said, so that's good. Come. The ladies have prepared a meal for us. You can come back and work later." Ragen waited for Roane to stand, not prepared to be swept close to his heart and held there. She liked the strength that she felt in his arms and the strength of his character.

Roane stared down at the face upturned to his before he once more gave into an impulse and kissed her not once but twice. Ragen didn't back away from him, he found, instead responding. That gave him hope that just maybe she had feelings for him as well.

"Okay. So we eat. Jerome has word?" He didn't release her despite his father appearing in the doorway, his mouth opening to call them to come for a meal before he snapped it closed, a soft smile lighting that man's face. Young love, he thought, wrapping an arm around Sofi who had followed him.

"Son?" Soft finally spoke, not wanting to be needing to. "Come and eat. Then we want to spend time in prayer. Your friends have all gathered here as well. Jerome has some answers for us."

"He does, does he, Mom?" Roane grinned at his parents before he walked towards them, not letting go of his lady love. "Then, that's what we do. Are Slavin and Nickol here as well? They've tried to help.:

"They are, son." Rourke's hand on his son's shoulder stopped the younger man, allowing the two ladies to walk ahead of them. "I know that you've prayed through your feelings. You don't have to say anything. Come and find me later. I have your great-grantdmother's ring that she left for you so many years ago."

Roane blinked. He had forgotten that over the years. Tears momentarily blinded him. He had loved that lady and been loved in return.

Two hours later, Jerome looked up from where he had had his head bowed as they had prayed and searched the faces in the crowded room. Everyone who could be there was there. He nodded to John, who was still struggling to understand the whys of what had happened.

"Okay, people." Jerome's voice cut through the chatter and brought all eyes to him. "I can tell what I can. There are some things that will stay undisclosed until the time of trial. I can say that all of the ones we have arrested are now turning on their leader. He doesn't stand a chance of getting off with anything.

"Smith was all that you thought, Roane, and more. He held a grudge against you since grade one as you suspected. Why was that? We can't rightly figure it out completely. We do know that at some point, he connected with Ragen and decided that she would be used to bring you to your knees and become involved in crime. He was the one who shadowed her and then called you. We have finally been able to trace the phones that he used to do that. He wasn't really that bright. Ragen? You did nothing to warrant what happened to you. You were just someone that he chose to use. Roane, you're asking why. I know that you are." Jerome grinned briefly at the laughter that spilled through the room. "Going back to before you started school, Smith watched you from what we term as the bad side of town. His father cheated regularly on his mother and so did his mother. They were both into drugs and were alcoholics. For some reason, he decided that you should help him. He is not clear on why as a young child he thought this but that anger and jealousy drove him through the years to become involved deeper and deeper in crime. I think at one point, your father had investigated something he had been involved him and had reported him. He skipped town before he could be charged. Rourke, I won't name the person and I'm not sure that you would even remember now as it was fifteen or more years ago. But the rage that filled him? It overflowed in many ways. There were times that he was very close to you and you just missed being injured or even dying. God was protecting you." Jerome answered what questions that he could before he was on his feet, heading away from the house, John at his side.

"I don't get why me, Jerome." John was still puzzled at that.

"Just because you were friends with Roane." Jerome paused, his head tilting back as he studied the clouds scudding across the sky. "You are good friends with Roane and he didn't have that kind of friendship. He thought that by hurting you he would hurt Roane."

John watched as Jerome walked away before he too walked away. He needed to be alone to absorb what had been said in the room and what he had been told in an official manner.

Late that afternoon, Ragen wandered the back yard. She was still trying to understand the rage that had led to her fleeing from town to town and the events that followed. She shook her head just as she felt an arm around her. Roane had found her and claimed her once more as his own.

"Okay, darling?" Roane just stood, holding his lady, waiting for just what he wasn't sure. He knew that it would take time for them both to feel safe and free once more. He looked up, thanking God that they were free once more to go on with their lives. He just didn't know if Ragen would stay or leave.

"I am, Roane. And you?" Ragen studied the tall man holding her, knowing that she had grown to love him and didn't want to leave. She would not stay, however, unless he asked her to.

"All's right in my world once more. I have life, joy, and the lady I love here with me." Roane was not really listening to what he said but Ragen was. She looked at him in surprise and then hugged him before she moved away, fatigue hitting her hard and fast.

Roane let her walk away, knowing that she was not going all that far from him. He too was exhausted, needing to seek his rest but wanting to find his prayer corner first. He had a lot to be thankful for that night. He chose to rejoice, finding joy in life once more

Three months later, Ragen turned from where she had been filing paperwork for Rourke. She had agreed to work for him and his sons in the paralegal office, choosing at that point not to work for Roane. It had been a deliberate decision of wanting to keep her work life separate from the life that she was finding with Roane outside of office hours.

"All set, Ragen?" Ryley grinned at her. "Off you go. I think Roane is here and waiting for you. We're all heading out early today." He was off himself, heading to find his own sweetheart. All of the siblings had settled with the loves of their lives, Roane and Ragen the last to acknowledge their feelings for one another.

Roane turned as Ragen's hand landed on his back, simply sweeping her into a hug, kissing her before he stood back and reached for her hand. His free hand was raised to his father as that man locked the doors behind them, Rourke watched the couple before nodding. They've come to some conclusion, he decided, and headed to find Sofi. Maybe she could tell him what the conclusion was. She had just laughed at him that morning when he asked her.

Roane reached once more for Ragen's hand as they headed for the river and the boardwalk that ran along its banks. It was a favourite spot for them to spend time, rain or shine or even snow.

"Happy, darling?" Roane grinned down at her, thinking how beautiful she was.

"I am, sweetheart. And I know that you are. What did you accomplish today?" She laughed softly as he made a face at her. "You did accomplish something, didn't you?"

"I did. I spoke with both John and Jerome. They tell me that Smith has finally agreed to the plea deal. He'll go away for the rest of his life, given his crimes. We don't have to testify."

"That's so wonderful. God did hear our pleas and answer them." Ragen reached to hug him before she walked ahead of him, turning to back to face him. "I am glad that we choose joy in all of this. It could have really brought us down. Instead, God has been there for us, protecting us, and helping us to find His joy and happiness in this."

"He did that, darling." Roane reached for her left hand, his finger on her ring finger. "I love you so much, Ragen. I was so afraid that you would leave me or else you would die. Will you be my darling for the rest of our lives and walk beside me as the help meet God has chosen for me?"

Ragen listened to him, her heart in her eyes, clouded as they were with her tears. Her mouth opened and closed before she simply hugged him and then watched as he placed an emerald ring on her finger. He had already told her to story of it.

"I will, sweetheart. I will. God brought us together. He had this planned for us. And as we go forward, no matter what we face, we will choose His joy."

Roane reached to kiss his sweetheart and then with an arm around her, walked her along the path. His family would not be surprised, he knew, but as the last one to settle with their life mates, he wanted some time with his darling Ragen to just take in that she had agreed to be his for life. His eyes raised to the sky as he once more thanked God for His protection in what they had faced.

Thank you for picking up Roane and Ragen's story, book two in the series, It has taken time to write, simply due to some health issues that I have been struggling with that made writing difficult.

Finding joy in our circumstances? We are told to rejoice at all time and that joy comes in the morning. We are all facing difficulties and events that can sap our strength and take our joy. God can restore that to us. It is hard to find joy when you're down or circumstances and events are such that they drive you to your knees in despair. Put your hand in God's and ask Him daily to restore your joy.

Once more, characters have walked into the series. Abe and Emma and his team are in *His Guardians*. Richard is in *His Protectors*. Don is in *His Defenders*. My characters just can't stay out of anyone else's stories. But I enjoy bringing them in. They always help to move the story line alone. Bill and his wife, Andrew and his wife, the four from Mistletoe, and other hinted at all shared adventures that others just had to walk into.

God bless each one of you as you walk this path called Life. Choose joy as your daily companion.

Ronna